PUFFIN BOOKS

LAPALEBOMBO

An African Paradise

Enter the wonderful world of LapaLebombo and discover a paradise of African wildlife. Here, animals, birds, reptiles and sea creatures live together, following their instincts and the ancient laws of nature into many exciting adventures.
　　A warthog family graze happily by the water's edge, until the largest piglet is suddenly snatched by Old Wily, the crocodile. Sheba and her pack of hyaenas stalk Angus, the ageing nyala bull, while Thandiwe, leader of a herd of elephants, tries to control her naughty young calf Nandi. Leopard Ngigwe forms an unlikely partnership with Mother Jackal, and the enchanting little blue duiker Piti eventually finds a mate.
　　This vast and beautiful area is threatened, though, by the activities of humans. Roads and fences divide the land and ploughed fields creep across the open veld. Can the animals escape from this invasion? And what does the arrival of a pair of young two-legs hold in store for the Wild Ones of LapaLebombo?
　　Here is a beautifully written tapestry of stories, weaving together a wealth of fascinating information and all the mystery and magic of the African plains.

LAPALEBOMBO

An African Paradise

Gill Bosonetto

PUFFIN BOOKS

PUFFIN BOOKS
Published by the Penguin Group
27 Wrights Lane, London W8 5TZ, England
Viking Penguin, a division of Penguin Books USA Inc, 375 Hudson Street,
New York, New York 10014, USA
Penguin Books Australia Ltd, Ringwood, Victoria, Australia
Penguin Books Canada Ltd, 10 Alcorn Avenue, Toronto, Ontario, Canada M4V 3B2
Penguin Books (NZ) Ltd, 182-190 Wairau Road, Auckland 10, New Zealand
Penguin Books South Africa (Pty) Ltd, Pallinghurst Road, Parktown, South Africa 2193
Penguin Books South Africa (Pty) Ltd, Registered Offices:
20 Woodlands Drive, Woodmead, Sandton 2128

First published in South Africa by Puffin Books 1996
1 3 5 7 9 10 8 6 4 2

Copyright © Gill Bosonetto, 1996
Illustrations copyright © Ulla Blake, 1996

The moral right of the author has been asserted

Cover and text illustrations and design by Ulla Blake
Typeset in 13 point Baskerville by Graphco (Tvl) (Pty) Ltd
Printed and bound by The Rustica Press,
Old Mill Road, Ndabeni, Western Cape

D5044

Except in the United States of America, this book is sold subject to the condition that it shall not, by way of trade or otherwise, be lent, re-sold, hired out, or otherwise circulated without the publisher's prior consent in any form of binding or cover other than that in which it is published and without a similar condition including this condition being imposed on the subsequent purchaser

ISBN 0 140 38244 5

AUTHOR'S NOTE

LapaLebombo is a fantasy place set in the actual wonderland of Maputaland. Called 'Paradise Under Pressure' by Alan Mountain in his book of that title, the area is a vast region rich in diverse and often unique plant and animal life. It lies in the northern Kwa-Zulu Natal region of South Africa, between the Lebombo and Ubombo Mountains and the Indian Ocean. Its northern border is Mozambique and the southernmost point of the triangle is the St Lucia Estuary. Included in the area are several nature reserves, such as Mkuze and False Bay Game Reserves and Sodwana Bay National Park. Its future as an environmental treasure-house is threatened by the usual pressures of population growth and industrial development.

Only with careful conservation-oriented management can the region remain the tropical paradise it still is today. One possible solution for the future of at least part of the area is its declaration as a World Heritage Site, which would give it internationally-recognised special conservation status.

Although this story is intended for children, through them it may bring the plight of Maputaland and all other environmentally-threatened areas to the attention of a much wider audience. Above all, though, I hope that it entertains and delights its readers.

Some of the names given to the animals are drawn either from their scientific or local African language names. While the story is a flight of imagination, I have tried to let the animals behave true to their nature.

Thanks to my husband and parents, who made the writing of this story possible.

Gill Bosonetto
February 1996

For Tim, Paul and Ashley, and the animals

There is a special place in Africa, a place called LapaLebombo. It is named after a vast range of magical mountains that surround the bushy hills and valleys of what used to be called Zululand, where in days long ago chiefs and soldiers fought many battles to decide who would be king. But in the time of this story, the humans who lived in the area had made peace and were living happily enough together, looking after their children and their homes, and generally making life comfortable for themselves. The only trouble was that now, people were able to produce more babies and live longer, and spend more time growing crops and keeping stock like cattle and goats, and this was making the animals of LapaLebombo very worried.

The area might have been blessed with wide rivers and miles of plants and trees of every kind, but the animals were finding that whenever they roamed away from their usual stomping grounds, they ran into roads or fences or ploughed-up fields or, worse still, the humans themselves.

And while the humans looked after their cattle, goats and hens, they did not protect or respect the wild animals of LapaLebombo. On the contrary, they would often hunt down those animals for their meat or their hides, and even for their horns, and sometimes just for fun. They would also trap and kill them as punishment for stealing their stock, or simply out of fear that they *would* steal their stock. And if a human were even so much as to see a creature like the fearsome black mamba, a long silvery grey snake with a poison that could kill the bravest warrior in one bite, or the spotted golden serval, which was blamed for raiding poultry runs, he would hack it to death without pausing once to wonder if this was really necessary.

So the Wild Ones, as all the free animals of LapaLebombo were known, were wondering where they could go to escape the slow but steady takeover of their territory by the humans. They began to talk about the problem amongst themselves.

'Even if our share of the land doesn't grow smaller as the humans' share grows bigger, there are many strange things showing up in the rivers these days,' warned Old Wily, the craftiest crocodile whose forefathers had existed since before the beginning of our time. 'Such things spoil a creature's food and drink, and will lead to a sorry end for us all!'

Old Wily was talking about the foul-smelling chemicals and waste products that the humans washed away into the rivers, and the plastic bags, bottles, cans and boxes that came floating down on the water. They often got stuck, clogging up the streams so that fish and other small animals were trapped in dirty little dams to die.

As you already know, the place of LapaLebombo was flanked on one side by a mountain range that reached as high as the heavy storm clouds of summer. The Wild Ones had thought of trekking over these mountains, but the rhinoceros and hippopotamus both doubted they could ever climb so high, and the crocodiles and other creatures of the broad lazy rivers wouldn't dare venture so far from the water. They also had to consider those high fences blocking their way at various points.

The animals also had no idea of what lay on the other side of the Lebombo Mountains. The bird who flew the farthest inland and knew most about the countryside, Yellow-billed Kite, could tell them only that it was very dry and flat on the other side. He had once met a distant cousin who claimed that not too far north, one came to a place where there were no trees, no rivers and no valleys; just mountains of concrete and glass, pathways paved with something hot and black, and strange hills the colour of gold, where nothing grew at all.

His cousin had spoken (in a most matter-of-fact way) of rabbits and hares and other small game being mowed down by streams of monstrous loud trucks that travelled the man-made paths, and had suggested to Kite that if he really wanted to live well, he should follow him north where 'the pickin's are easy, man, if ya know where ta go an' whatta do.'

After listening to the tale in quiet horror, the Wild Ones had resolved never to set their course north, even if the humans ended up killing every last one of them.

Scattered all over the land south of LapaLebombo were settlements of humans called villages, and about a hundred kilometres away was a big town. Beyond that, the Wild Ones had been told, was a huge city on the sea, and there was another city in a valley one hundred kilometres inland from there. In between were farms of sugarcane, sisal, cattle, fruit and vegetables, which had been stripped bare of the natural bush and trees that supported the animals of the Wild.

It seemed like the animals had no choice but to stay where they were.

'So how are we going to make LapaLebombo safe for our

children, and their children's children?' asked Camilla the giraffe, who with her long neck was used to seeing far and wide, and wanted to see into the future too. 'It's only a matter of time before the humans find that all the vast land they already have is not enough, and try to take over ours as well.'

The others nodded in agreement, remembering tales of how their ancestors had ranged in great herds over the countryside without meeting fences or boundaries. They had travelled north and south freely, choosing to move with the seasons and follow the rains. Some of the older animals also remembered hearing of a terrible time many seasons past when the humans seemed to have declared war on all Wild Ones. They had come in droves with guns and shot everything that moved. Some said this was because the humans were trying to rid the area of the tsetse fly, which carried a disease that was killing their livestock, and also made people sick so they slept all the time. Who was to say the humans wouldn't get it into their heads to come after all their kind again with their terrible fire sticks? Those that had survived to produce the offspring who now roamed LapaLebombo had been very lucky. Next time, perhaps none would survive.

The animals couldn't decide how to protect themselves. They were not to know that in the big cities of the south, some humans were discussing the very same problem – how to make the Wild Ones safe for their children and their children's children to watch and enjoy.

A little blue duiker called Piti was particularly distressed by all this talk of the dangers which threatened LapaLebombo. Being the smallest of the antelope, as well as very shy, he had been too scared to ask the larger animals how long it would be before the humans took their land. He didn't understand that it would be a gradual process everyone would barely notice until it was too late.

Piti hid in the thick undergrowth near a watering hole the whole day, thinking about his future. He felt especially lonely because, unlike most of the other blue duikers of LapaLebombo, he had not yet found a mate and sired a young one. He was so small, and the females seemed to overlook him in favour of stronger bucks.

When the sun had at last sunk to its knees for a drink at the waterhole, and then slipped into the earth for its night's slumber, Piti ventured out of the forest. Very cautiously he stretched out one leg, then the next, and shook his little head. He had two horns just above and between his ears, but they were short and lay almost flat on his head, offering little protection against a predator. He also had to make sure the eagles were gone to roost, and that there were no hungry pythons lying in wait.

Slowly he stepped towards the water, sniffing the air for animal scents. He could smell a few zebra, giraffe and warthog, but was not concerned about them. He knew they were also off to the watering hole for their last drink of the day. He sniffed again. Something new was in the air.

'I think it's a female duiker, a blue one, like me,' he said to himself. 'But I bet she already has a mate...'

He stood waiting, ears pricked, at the water's edge. Out of the darkness of the trees to his right came the form of another blue duiker. He was right, it was a female. Piti now waited for the male he thought would be sure to follow. The female, who had the cutest black smile lines below her eyes that he had ever seen, went straight to the water. Without even glancing about her, she began to sip. Piti searched the trees for another duiker. Nothing.

With his heart pounding in his chest, he picked his way over to within a few steps of the female, and dipped his head to drink. His thoughts were racing.

'What if she thinks I'm too forward? What if her mate is on his way? What if she thinks I'm too small? What if... what if...?'

In his excitement, he forgot to worry as usual about whether some predator was lurking behind him as he drank. All he could think of was the female, and her sweet scent, and what he should say to her before she left.

Before he had a chance to say anything, the female stopped drinking, lifted her head to look at him, and asked, 'Do you know of a safe place where I could browse tonight, young buck?'

Piti couldn't believe his ears. This gorgeous satiny doe with the velvety nose and enormous, dark, liquid eyes needed protection, and a new browsing spot, which meant she needed a mate!

Lifting his head high and puffing out his chest, Piti turned to her.

'My dear, I know of a grove in the thicket that is safe, but has no beauty. If you would follow me there, it will have that too,' he replied, his skinny legs quivering with hope.

The doe snickered, delighted at the compliment.

'I hope your charm was not taught to you by our smooth-skinned legless cousins,' she laughed, referring to the snakes of LapaLebombo.

'Dear lady, come with me, before we are dinner for something larger than our legless cousins,' said Piti, who suddenly remembered how long they had been exposed at the water's edge.

'Do you know of a safe place where I could browse tonight, young buck?'

'May I?' asked the doe. Piti was later to learn she was named Petals because she had once been found eating the flowers from a plant, instead of its fruit and leaves.

Quickly Piti turned back to the thicket, and Petals followed close at his heels. Once in the shelter of the dark bushes, Piti turned to look once more at the twilight that had brought him such luck. A deep red smeared the sky as night was falling, and he was just in time to see the outline of what he guessed was a lion leading his pride down to the water to drink. With a swish of their stumpy tails, he and Petals leaped further into the thicket and safely into Piti's hiding place, where they settled down very cosily together for the night.

On the eastern side of LapaLebombo lay the vast, shining blue Sea. Many of the Wild Ones had seen it, the others had heard about it in stories told over and over again at the waterholes. If you travelled south-east through the thickets on the sides of the hills that sloped gently towards the lakes called Hopeful Bay and the Sea of Gold, whose waters you could not drink, you came suddenly to the edge of a cliff. From that high point you could see water stretching west and inland from the Indian Ocean almost to the mountains. The animals thought of this estuary in the south as the beginning of the end of the world. Beyond the fingers of land that separated the lakes from the sea you could see only a line of blue as wide and flat as the sky itself.

It was at Hopeful Bay and the Sea of Gold that many of the Wild Ones met the creatures of the sea, who swam through the deep mouth of the estuary into its waters, made salty by the incoming ocean tides.

One day, Old Wily, who was the largest crocodile, was patrolling the coarse-sanded shore with his lazy, silent crawl when he spied a delicious-looking pink flamingo wading several metres away in the water. In his most artful way, he lay down still as a log, narrowed his eyes into tiny slits and held open his scissor-like jaws. He stayed like this for so long that even the sharp-eyed malachite kingfisher thought he had dozed off in the midday sun. As Flamingo stepped closer and closer, resting first one long leg and then the other while searching for juicy crabs near the shore, Old Wily breathed slower and slower, biding his time. Just when Flamingo came within one crocodile length of his quivering nostrils, he lunged at her legs, snapping his jaws with all his might. With the speed of a darting fish, Flamingo flapped her wings and flew high into the sky. Old Wily was left floundering in a deep water channel – and to his great alarm – face to face with the toothy grin and button-like eyes of Grey Shadow, a Zambezi shark. He was the most feared of all sharks who cruised the LapaLebombo coast because he so often ventured inland.

'Er, e-e-excuse me,' stuttered Old Wily, who was smart enough to let sharks rule the sea and crocodiles stick to terrorising the rivers. 'Just l-leaving, Grey Shadow,' he added.

Grey Shadow glanced fleetingly at Old Wily. Then, because he was much more interested in a school of threadfin that had just slipped by, he jerked his body away and headed off for deeper waters and richer fishing grounds. A solitary eel-catfish snickered quietly to itself as it honed in on a crab disturbed from the muddy lake floor by the sudden action.

Old Wily, never one to be easily embarrassed, snapped his jaws a few more times, swished his powerful tail and heaved his scaly body back on to the shore. He was already convincing himself that all he had meant to do was scare away Grey Shadow. Flamingo, from a safe distance across the lake, knew better. But soon she too was back at foraging for food, her brush with the jaws of doom forgotten. A flock of pelicans that had struck out raucously into the air at the sound of the disturbance soon settled their fish-heavy bodies back on the water, at rest for the day.

Most of the encounters between the Wild Ones of the land and those of the sea were more pleasant, and some were memorable. The tale the Wild Ones like to repeat around the watering holes is the story of the dolphins and the warthog.

Among the various species of Wild Ones was a family of warthog: mother, father and three piglets. Warthog are not usually thought of as pretty: they have strange faces with big nostrils and large curly tusks at the end of their snouts, warts jutting out the sides, and funny little tufts of spiky hair on their heads. They are quite sociable fellows, though, often seen in the company of buck, or giraffe, or zebra, or even the massive rhinoceros, grazing peacefully together.

There was a special place that this warthog family liked to visit which was not fancied by the others, for good reason. Between the sheer cliffs overlooking Hopeful Bay and the waters of the lake itself was a flat stretch of land where the river took its laziest route to the sea, wandering this way and that in slow, generous curves. The grasses that grew on these marshes were the most tender, juicy-tasting plants Old Man Warthog had ever sampled.

Now, while the other animals of LapaLebombo agreed the grazing down on the flats was very good, they also knew that there was a great danger in straying towards the river mouth.

As you know, the shoreline of Hopeful Bay was a favourite hunting ground of the crocodiles, but even more dear to them was the wide river bank. If a hoofed animal strayed too far or stayed too long here, it was bound to find itself sinking into the mud without much chance of escape should some large, snapping jaws come its way. Once the crocodile had seized the poor animal, he would drag it into the river and under the water where it would end its happy days as crocodile dinner.

One particularly hot summer day, Old Man Warthog and family were on the marsh enjoying a late afternoon graze. The largest of the piglets, whom the animals named Whistle because of his ear-piercing squeal, was the bravest and the hungriest. Despite the warnings of his papa, he rooted around in ever-widening circles until, lo and behold, he was out of sight of the others. To his horror, he began sinking ever so quickly into the muddy shore of the river!

Whistle let out his loudest cry, shrieking, 'Mama, Mama, I'm stuck... HELP!'

'Oh Papa, quick!' screamed Mama Warthog. 'Whistle is in the mud somewhere – help me find him, and hurry!'

Whistle's father, mother, brother and sister all flew into a wild gallop, their short tails sticking straight into the air and their grunts and snorts attracting Wild Ones from miles around. Sharing the poor sight of all warthogs, none of them could actually see Whistle, who in any case was well hidden by the long grasses of the marsh.

The little ones were too frightened to go near the river in case they also got stuck, so they scattered in different directions, and Mama was in such a panic that she just ran back and forth on the spot. Old Man Warthog was the only one who headed in the right direction.

From where he was floundering in the mud, Whistle heard

all the commotion, and he squealed higher and higher.

'Over here, Papa, here,' he cried in terror.

But alas, just as he saw Papa was close enough to catch him before his belly sank under the mud, he felt a terrible burning pain as something snatched at his leg. He realised that it wasn't Papa, but Crocodile Mcrunchu.

Old Man Warthog was just in time to see Whistle being pulled into the river and under the water. He skidded to a halt at the river's edge, and let out a howl of anguish as he saw his son's head bobbing in the water.

'Don't give up, Whistle,' he shouted. 'Fight him! Mcrunchu has no patience – you might get away.'

But Old Man Warthog's words were lost in the wind that had suddenly sprung up. As he ran up and down the side of the river calling to Whistle, he felt heavy drops of rain and heard a sudden crash of thunder. In seconds, the warthogs found themselves in the middle of a furious downpour of rain. Mama had no choice but to round up her remaining children and herd them off to safety, leaving her frantic mate behind.

'Oh, Whistle, keep fighting!' cried Old Man Warthog.

'You mean horrible crocodile,' he yelled at Mcrunchu, whose swishing tail he could just make out in the water.

But once again his cries were in vain, and he found himself rapidly getting into danger as his own hooves began to sink in the mud and his view of the river became blurred by rain. He too had no choice but to head for higher ground. Only just in time, because no sooner had he scrambled up the pathway to the cliff than a huge wave of water came roaring down the river. It spilled over the flats, washing everything but the stoutest trees before it and towards the bay.

In abject misery, Old Man Warthog stood with the many

other animals who had come to watch the drama from the top of the cliff. All they could see now was swirling water and mud flowing into the lake, where it tossed and churned in the huge waves that were pounding the shoreline.

In silence the Wild Ones looked at the Warthog family. Each parent there felt the loss that Old Man Warthog and

Mama were feeling. The young ones looked away, remembering the times they had disobeyed their elders, and thinking how lucky they had been if all they'd had was a head butt or a nip from their mothers for their actions. The warthog piglets bleated pitifully, and squeezed as close to Mama's side as they could. All the animals were soaked as they stood in the pouring rain, but few paid attention to their wet coats. They just stood and waited.

Realising he was expected to say something before the others would return to their business, Old Man Warthog turned his back on the lake and faced the gathering.

'Bless his precious soul,' he said of Whistle. 'And thanks to those of you who would have helped if you could.'

And then he nudged Mama Warthog and signalled her and the piglets to follow him. Shaking their heads in sympathy, the Wild Ones watched as they walked away.

Just as quickly as the rain had come, it ceased. A brilliant rainbow appeared, its feet planted in the grass of the marshes at either end of Hopeful Bay. The few Wild Ones who were looking out to sea wondered at the glory of the colours so soon after tragedy had struck.

Suddenly they heard a shriek. Fish Eagle, who had soared out over the flats as soon as the rain stopped, had seen something. Lying motionless on the sandy shore of the bay was a small shape, the browny grey colour of a warthog. As he circled lower, he made out a thin tail, with a bedraggled tuft of hair at the end. And as he flew lower still, he saw the closed slanty eyes atop a broad snout that told him the shape was definitely what he thought it was.

'It's Whistle!' he cried.

Old Man Warthog was leading his dejected family to the abandoned aardvark hole that was their home at night when he heard Fish Eagle's cry. He stopped dead in his tracks. Mama and the piglets, who were following with their heads hanging low, bumped into Papa and each other.

'What is it, Papa?' asked Mama Warthog.

'Wait here,' ordered Papa, who was afraid of what Fish Eagle might have found. He trotted back to the cliff edge, down the path to the flats and towards the spot on the shoreline that Fish Eagle was indicating. Too anxious to listen to any orders, Mama followed Papa at a distance, and behind her came the piglets.

As he neared the shore, Papa knew by the scent that it was Whistle's body lying there so still. With a heavy heart, he trotted up to the little shape and gently nudged at it with his short tusks. As he rolled Whistle's body over, Papa heard a splutter, then a cough, and then a dreadful retching sound as a spout of water came out of Whistle's mouth. Caught by surprise, Old Man Warthog jumped back for a moment. In the background, Mama froze in her tracks and the piglets cowered behind her.

Whistle's body began to shake. Then his eyes flew open, and he twisted on to his stomach. He shook his head, coughed again, and rose shakily to his feet.

'He's alive!' screamed Papa. Mama came running to his side, and together they pranced a circle around Whistle. Whistle gave a weak little bleat, then collapsed on the sand once more. Mama raced to his side, nuzzling him with all the love she could muster.

'Are you all right? Come to Mama,' she crooned as Whistle leant his shivering body against her. The piglets ran up to Whistle as well, and began to lick at his face, squealing with happiness at seeing their big brother again.

'Well, come on everybody,' said Old Man Warthog gruffly. 'Let's get the poor fellow to our hole where he can rest. His one hind leg looks rather hurt, but we'll help him along. It's getting dark, and we can't stay here. He can tell us what happened tomorrow.'

And so he hurried the others up, pushing at them until he had them forming a huddle around Whistle. Together they lifted and prodded the wounded creature up the cliff and all the way to their home in the thicket.

Although a watery-looking sun had long since sunk behind the hills, the rest of the Wild Ones used the remaining twilight to watch the procession. A great cheer went up when the warthogs reached their hole and Whistle let out an exhausted grunt of relief. The Wild Ones were only to find out the next day how Whistle had survived his ordeal with Mcrunchu and the fury of the storm.

3

At the first sign of light the next day, Wild Ones from far and wide were gathering in a clearing in the thicket. Word had spread through the night that the fierce Crocodile Mcrunchu had been thwarted by a three-year-old warthog, of all creatures. Everyone wanted to hear the tale from the little hero himself.

Winston, the white rhinoceros who always seemed to appoint himself Speaker at these animal indabas, or meetings, snorted twice to bring the chattering group to attention.

Mungo, one of a huge family of banded mongoose that had taken up position in a kooboo-berry tree with a great view of the clearing, was chittering loudly at a hadeda for standing in his way.

'Look out, you big noisy bird,' he said, 'you're blocking my view. Move it!' He was very cocky for someone his size, but excitement makes the usually faint-hearted brave, and curiosity can make the most cautious creatures daring. The other mongooses joined in as they jostled for the best position and the twittering became almost deafening.

Taking a deep breath, Winston let out a very deep, warning growl. The sound rumbled through the clearing, and suddenly everyone was still. After a pause to make sure the quiet would last, Winston began.

'We have here today the most remarkable thing. That is, er, we have in our midst a small creature that in the ordinary nature of things, er, that is to say, the way fate normally takes its course, er, would have by now been long digested in the bowels of one of the ancient species of reptile, the crocodile. But instead, he sits here with his happy parents and we wait on him, er, for an er, yes, explanation of his lucky escape.'

Whistle stood and looked around at all the Wild Ones, whose eyes were fixed firmly on him. He opened his mouth to say something, and all that came out was one of his squeakiest squeals. The animals began to titter.

With more force than he intended, Old Man Warthog nudged Whistle and hissed, 'Get on with it then, boy.'

With his back legs still rather unsteady, Whistle almost fell over. He began again.

'Well, uh, I was just trying to get something really good to eat when I got stuck in the mud, and, uh, I was just calling to Mama to help get me out, and then suddenly I felt something pulling at my back leg... and it was very sore,' he stammered.

He saw the Wild Ones nodding encouragement for him to go on and so, drawing a deep breath, he continued.

'I knew it was Crocodile Mcrunchu, because when I turned I saw the deep round scar he has on the side of his head, which Mama said he got when he was a baby and he was bothering Hippopotamus Hothead, and he got bitten. Uh, then the next thing I knew, I was in the river under the water, and I was so scared I couldn't even scream for Papa or Mama any more, and I was just fighting to breathe but Mcrunchu kept pulling me back under.' Whistle's little body began to tremble as he relived his fear.

The quail and francolin that were huddled together closest to Whistle began to cluck and tut-tut with consternation.

'Poor child,' tutted Constance Quail, 'perhaps we should wait a few days before he tells his tale.'

'Nonsense, fiddlesticks,' spluttered Papio, the nearest chacma baboon. 'Can't you see he needs to tell the story, and get it out of his system?'

Winston, who had been looking suspiciously like he was nodding off to sleep, jerked his head up with a snort.

'Continue, boy,' he said to Whistle, 'and would the rest of you kindly BE QUIET.'

'Well, uh, as I was saying,' Whistle went on, 'I was just thinking I had seen Papa for the last time ever, and all I could see was the cloudy grey sky above the river as I took my last big breath, when there was a crashing sound, and a huge wall of water seemed to come from nowhere. Mcrunchu must have been just as startled as I was, because I felt him let go of my leg, and I kicked as hard as I could to get away. I think he would have grabbed me again, because he is very quick, and his long jaws were still very close. But as I kicked, the wall of water seemed to pick me up and roll me over and over until I didn't know which was sky and which was water.'

The Wild Ones leaned forward as one body, and Whistle began to enjoy himself.

'I remember seeing grey one second, then yellow-brown, then green, then grey, and hearing the roar of waves and seeing white foamy water. I couldn't touch the ground or see the banks of the river. I think that was because by now I was washed out into the lake, and I knew that pretty soon I'd be beyond the lake and in the faraway sea. Then nobody would ever be able to find me, and I would surely drown.

'I could hear the thunder and see the bright flashes in the sky which make the summer rains so fierce, and I wished I had never strayed so far away from the others... even if the grazing was better. I promise I won't do it again, Papa.'

'Oh, what happened next?' cried Zorilla, the striped polecat, who normally ventured out only at night, and was growing impatient with Whistle's long story. 'Tell us how you got back here,' he snapped.

The animals close to Zorilla backed away. They knew only too well the vile scent the woolly black-and-white striped Zorilla could spray if he became annoyed, and none wanted to be in the line of fire. There was a small flutter as some backed too close to Porcupine, and Porcupine rattled his quills in warning.

'Well, the funny thing is I don't know for sure what happened next,' continued Whistle. There was a groan from the audience, the birds in the trees began chattering, and Winston the rhinoceros had to clear his throat again to bring everyone to order.

'Well, what I mean is, one minute I was struggling in the waves, and the next minute, I felt something under my belly lifting me up out of the water. I felt very calm all of a sudden. Even if I'd wanted to get away I couldn't have... I was so exhausted and just hung on. I looked around and saw something big and grey in the water next to me. I thought, Oh no, now a shark's got me, and I'll never get away, but somehow I wasn't afraid.

'And then another silvery shape came up next to me. I saw its long round nose, and a strange hole that was in its head, and its eyes, which were friendly-looking. It came up to me and bumped me, but gently, and didn't try to bite me at all. I realised I was slung over the nose of one of these unusual sharks, and it was taking me towards the shore. The other one kept swimming around us, and he would leap out of the water and come down on the other side of us, as though we were playing catch or something.'

'Dolphins!' exclaimed Fish Eagle. 'Those weren't sharks, silly, they were dolphins. Wonder what they were doing in the lake? Must've come in with the rough seas and high tide. Lucky you, young man, lucky you.'

'Dolphins?' asked Old Man Warthog. 'What are they?'

Several seagulls, who had flown inland when they'd seen the Wild Ones gathering at dawn, screeched with amusement.

'You ain't heard o' dolphins?' they cried. 'He ain't heard o' dolphins,' they nudged each other.

Now, very few of the Wild Ones had heard of dolphins, but when they heard the laughter of the gulls, none of them dared say so.

'Dolphins, my dear man, are knights in shining armour – the heroes of the sea,' Fish Eagle answered Old Man Warthog. 'They are loved by all in the ocean, except perhaps the sharks, for they swim with the grace of birds and play with the fun of cubs. They breathe air through the hole in the head which Whistle saw because they are not fish, but mammals like you. They are also very clever, and no doubt they knew Whistle was in trouble. What did they do with you next, Whistle?'

'They swam with me to the shore, and as we reached shallow water they pushed me into a wave. I was washed on to the beach, where you found me, Fish Eagle, but I was too tired to move. Then I don't remember anything until I saw

'I was slung over the nose of one of these unusual sharks, and it was taking me towards the shore.'

Papa and Mama again.'

Old Man Warthog turned to Whistle. 'It does seem that you were very lucky to be rescued by the dolphin mammals of the sea, my boy. But don't ever trust that you will be blessed with the same luck in the future. Next time, stay where it's safe.

'And the rest of you,' he turned to his family, 'remember we will never graze on the marshes again.'

So the young Wild Ones learned a great respect for the ocean, the lake and the river, and that particular family of warthog never went down the cliff to graze on the flats after that. But they could often see Whistle gazing out from the edge of the cliff, searching the waters of the lake for a glimpse of the friendly dolphins who saved his life.

Some days after Whistle's encounter with the dolphins, two other animals were also about to meet at a waterhole behind the hill known as Leopard's Crest.

High in the branches of a beautiful flat-crowned acacia tree, a handsome leopard lay licking his paws. He had been lucky that night, having nabbed an adventuresome dassie that had strayed from the colony of almost a hundred dassies living in the rocky cliffs below Leopard's Crest. The dassie had been in search of some tasty looking herbs at the top of the cliff, and Leopard Ngigwe had wasted no time in pouncing on his prey as the long shadows of evening hid his advance.

Now, with his belly full, Ngigwe looked out over the dark veld with only a glimmer of interest in the movements he could detect in the long grass. He felt no great need to go chasing after the fast-moving impala he knew were there, nervously looking for shelter from the brilliant light of a rising full moon. He looked lazily at a group of trees where he could make out a gathering of larger antelope: probably nyala, perhaps even kudu. And in the distance he could make out the tall silhouettes of a herd of giraffe, whom even at his

Lowering his belly almost to the ground, so that he could crawl completely unnoticed. In the small circle of dust, he saw the strangest sight.

hungriest he never bothered to try and capture.

But suddenly a high 'whoop-hoop-hoop' cry pierced the peace of the night. Hyaena, thought Ngigwe. Someone else got lucky early tonight. Then the cry was followed by a new, strange sound, a long eerie 'aaaaa-na-ha-ha'.

Odd, thought Ngigwe, who by now was sitting up stiffly in the fork of the tree, his ears straining towards the sounds. I could swear that was a jackal, but never before have I heard one talk with hyaenas!

Very quietly, as is the way of the big cats, Ngigwe leaped out of his acacia tree and slowly crept through the tall grass towards the trees from where the hair-raising cries were coming. He heard again the voice of a hyaena – this time a low moan – then the jackal, 'njaaaaaa-ha-ha'.

Sounds like trouble, said Ngigwe to himself, and he bent his legs deeper, lowering his belly almost to the ground, so that he could crawl completely unnoticed. Very slowly he came to the edge of a ring of trees. In the small circle of dust, he saw the strangest sight.

There was the jackal he had heard, with its ears back and hair bristling, staring hard into the eyes of a hyaena. It was driving the hyaena backwards away from the carcass of an impala, probably left there earlier by lions. The hyaena had his raggedy tail tucked deep between his legs but was still protesting, growling and yelping even as he retreated. Ngigwe could see that the spotted hyaena was easily twice the size of the black-backed jackal, who in quick darts was snapping and snarling at the hyaena's face.

As soon as the jackal seemed to be sure the hyaena had been scared off, it snatched at the leg of the impala and galloped into the bushes, dragging the prize behind. The hyaena melted away into the darkness.

Amazed, Ngigwe decided to follow the jackal. Keeping a careful distance, he crept along the path the jackal made towards a little cave in a mound of sand and rocks nearby. He paused before the clearing next to the mound, and lay down to watch. Dropping the carcass, the jackal disappeared into the mouth of the cave and then re-emerged, followed by not one, not two, but seven little cubs.

Incredible! thought Ngigwe. Never before have I seen a hyaena chased off by such a small animal, especially one who must be a female, and never before have I seen so many little cubs together.

He licked his lips and flicked the tip of his long tail thoughtfully. Meanwhile the cubs leaped hungrily at the carcass, tearing at whatever flesh and bones they could reach as they clambered over each other. Gnawing on a thigh bone, Mother Jackal lay and watched her brood, unaware of Leopard Ngigwe's presence in the bushes.

Now Ngigwe had quite a dilemma.

His natural instinct as a leopard confronted by a litter of virtually helpless cubs was to gobble up at least a couple and perhaps drag one back to his tree for later. After all, Mother Jackal may have scared off a hyaena, but she was certainly no match for him and would never be able to protect all seven cubs at once. At the same time, Ngigwe had to admit to himself that he was rather impressed by Mother Jackal and her brood.

A gutsy little hussy, she is, he thought to himself. And a remarkable breeder – wonder who and where the father is...

Being a leopard, Ngigwe tended to hunt and live alone. He knew jackals did the same. Hyaenas, on the other hand, liked to gather in noisy, rumbustious packs. They even drove the big cats away from their own kills sometimes, Ngigwe remembered. And the way they let out those ghastly laughing sounds!

No, decided Ngigwe, with a shudder. I don't care much for those scrawny-necked dogs who have tried to copy my gorgeous spotted coat and ended up looking ridiculous. This lady at least has some class, with her cloak of black and her silver bib.

I think I'll leave her to her cubs. But first, he smiled to himself, I'll let her know how generous I am. She will learn that I am the true king of the bushveld, and she will always show me respect.

With that, he boldly paced through the fringe of bush surrounding Mother Jackal's den, stepped up to one of the cubs still busy tearing at the carcass, and swatted its behind with one of his huge paws. Then he turned to face its mother, who had leapt forward and then frozen at the sight of the leopard. Ngigwe raised his empty paw to his mouth, pretending to lick it, gave a little cough and flexed his claws instead, and then sauntered off back into the thicket.

Mother Jackal's hackles were raised in horror of what she feared was going to happen to her cubs and perhaps even herself. She stared after Ngigwe. Then, being the smart mother she was, she quickly gathered her thoughts and shooed her cubs into the old antbear hole she had made her home. There she lay, waiting in the case the leopard came back.

When she was sure he had really left them alone, Mother Jackal darted out to grab the carcass and chewed warily on what remained. As she swallowed the last few morsels, she resolved to be more watchful in future. And, as she considered her brush with the paws of disaster, she promised to do something for Ngigwe one day that would show her gratitude for his mercy.

For his part, Ngigwe made his way back to the giant acacia tree at Leopard's Crest, chuckling lightly as he recalled the look on Mother Jackal's face when he had showed himself to her.

'From now on, I shall think of that jackal as the Plucky One, or Ms Fiesty-pants,' he said.

Only the stars twinkling in the deep African sky heard him. But then the stars of the hot African night see and hear everything – many things that even to this day they keep to themselves.

5

The moon, as you know, starts out as a banana-shaped sliver one week, and then grows round and plump as an apple and bright as a silver coin in the next. As the third week passes by, it begins to wane, until in the last week of its travels around Planet Earth (which is where we and the Wild Ones live), you can hardly see it at all.

It is on those darkest of nights that the most mysterious things can happen. On one such night, a sudden loud 'whoo-hoo' rang out over the quiet northern reaches of LapaLebombo. The tallest giraffes stationed around a white stinkwood tree felt the cool swoosh of air as a spotted eagle owl dived between them, and then soared up again into the black velvet sky. The brief squeals of a cane rat faded into the distance. The giraffe stopped chewing for a moment, as if in sympathy for their much smaller four-legged cousin.

The silence of the summer night returned, broken only by the occasional fall of a hoof, or 'whe-whe-whe' of a nightjar. The spotted eagle owl, satisfied with his meal for the night, settled into his eyrie atop a fever tree growing close to the broad Mkuze River. He was just dozing off when a young marsh owl alighted on a branch next to him.

'Rufus, Rufus,' he called to the spotted eagle owl. 'Come quickly, I want to show you something!'

'Good heavens, young man,' Rufus hooted. 'Can't you see I'm at rest? What in the blazes has got you going? And the nerve too, to perch on my tree! Whoo-hoo.'

The younger owl, who was normally quite overawed by his larger spotted brother, hopped from leg to leg on his branch.

'I first looked for my family to come and see,' he creaked excitedly, 'but they must all be out hunting. I just had to have someone come witness what's going on. Please come, Rufus, or no one will ever believe me!'

'Now listen, Marshy,' warned the spotted eagle owl (who called all the marsh owls Marshy), 'you'd better have something good to show me or – ... Tell me, where do you want me to go?'

'Out to the sea, to the beaches,' cried Marshy. 'But do hurry, or they'll all be gone.'

To the sea! hooted Rufus. 'Are you mad, as well as cocky, young man? And whoooo will all be gone, may I ask?'

'The two-legs, and the flipper-feet,' replied a very agitated Marshy. 'Please come, now – I must see them again.'

And with that Marshy took off into the air, heading east to where Rufus knew the land met the Great Salt Waters of the rest of the world. Shaking his head in disbelief at what he was doing, Rufus launched himself after Marshy. He caught the lift of warm air coming inland from the sea, and pointed his sharp curved beak into the breeze.

Peering through the night sky, Rufus made out the distant sea-shore, glimmering faintly in the starlight. He could smell the fresh salty air, and hear the roar of the waves as they broke on the silvery sand. Ahead of him, Marshy flew in sweeping curves, heading seawards and slightly north.

'Better not be much longer,' grumbled Rufus to himself, not used to flying so far. He yawned, too. 'Hey Marshy,' he called, 'are we nearly there?'

'Almost, almost,' shrieked Marshy. 'But hush now, let's not scare them off.'

'Hmmfff,' replied Rufus.

He was just about to tell Marshy not to order him around, when the young marsh owl dropped into a wheeling dive and out of Rufus's sight. Rufus tilted his wings and circled down, finding himself on the fringe of the coastal bush and overlooking a broad flat beach. He perched in the branches of a thick red milkwood tree, and looked around.

Before him were small bobbing lights and, as his eyes adapted to the scene, he made out the moving bodies of several large creatures.

The two-legs! he thought. That's what Marshy was talking about. Very curious himself now, he leaned forward, staring hard at the sands, his eyes as wide as cut melons. The two-legs were carrying baskets, which every now and then they would put down and appear to fill with sand.

Moving to a tree closer to a group of two-legs, Rufus saw Marshy, who signalled to him to look at the ground. There Rufus saw yet another shape he had never come across before: a large bumpy rock with two pairs of moving bits on either side, and one larger round shape at the front. The whole thing was travelling up the beach. Then it stopped, and began to scrape a hole in the sand with its rear moving bits.

'It must be alive,' he whispered to Marshy.

'Oh yes it is,' squeaked Marshy. 'Wait till you see what the flipper-feet does next!'

With his words, the 'flipper feet' dropped some small pale

'It must be alive,' he whispered to Marshy.
'Oh yes it is,' squeaked Marshy. 'Wait till you see what the flipper-feet does next!'

rocks in the sand, then scuttled away, heading back for the sea. As Rufus looked harder, he saw the small rocks were like large bird eggs, and he realised that he was looking at the nest of this strange rock-like creature.

For its part, the 'flipper-feet' plunged into the waves, swimming off with its flippers looking like featherless wings flapping against the current.

Now Marshy, who spent a lot more time near waterways than did Rufus, had seen a similar creature before, in the deep Mkuze River.

'Turtles,' he hissed at Rufus. 'I've seen them swim in the river, but these must be sea turtles.'

They were in fact loggerhead turtles, coming ashore for their annual nest laying. In about two-and-a-half moon cycles the eggs would hatch; that is, if the nests remained undisturbed. The eggs were sometimes crushed by the wheels of beach buggies or tractors moving sand around, or trampled on by careless holidaymakers.

If they survived these dangers, thousands of newborn hatchlings would try to make their way to the water as quickly as possible. They would have to escape hungry birds dropping out of the sky (Rufus had no idea how tasty baby turtles were), and greedy ghost crabs scurrying out of holes in the sand. Once in the sea, they would have to swim as hard as they could to escape the mouths of the many fish who found them just as tempting and nutritious to eat. If they lived to grow up, the females would, like their mothers before them, return to the same beach to lay their own eggs. This would be after many years of swimming the vast waters along the southern coast of Africa.

'But what are the two-legs doing?' asked Rufus, who no longer felt so superior to Marshy.

He watched as the two-legs came out of hiding to go from nest to nest, gathering up the eggs with the sand they were putting into their baskets.

'They must be going to eat them,' said Rufus, nodding his head wisely.

'I don't know,' replied Marshy. 'I saw others earlier taking them away, and they were eating something else, out of bags. They didn't seem to want the eggs to eat.'

Marshy was right. The two-legs, or humans, were taking the eggs to another beach further south, which they would make a protected site, only disturbed by the normal forces of nature. Like the Wild Ones of LapaLebombo, these humans knew the creatures of the wild and of the sea were at risk without some kind of protection.

The two owls watched the process repeated hundreds of times. Turtles coming up to lay their eggs, two-legs waiting until they were gone and then scooping the eggs into baskets they carried away. Eventually, the faint light of dawn began to spread over the ocean. Rufus yawned for the first time since he had reached the beach.

'Marshy,' he mumbled, 'it's getting late – almost daybreak. I'll be setting off home now. If I don't get to sleep before the other twits wake up, I never will. They make such a racket in the trees!'

He was talking, of course, about the birds who feed and fly by day and sleep at night. An African dawn is filled with the clamorous song of thousands of birds busying themselves with catching the first worm, or pecking the juiciest fruit, before the sun climbs hot and high in the sky.

'I'm coming,' creaked Marshy, and the two birds took off into the fading dark, towards their homes.

'I'm glad you showed me the turtles,' Rufus said, just as he began nodding off to sleep on his perch. 'Although it will all seem like a dream when I wake up.'

Before Marshy had time to comment from his nearby roost, Rufus was asleep, his head tucked into his chest, looking like nothing more than a stump of old branch in his tree. As the first rays of sunlight shot through the eastern sky, Marshy's huge brown eyes dropped closed, and he too was in slumberland.

During the daytime, the hills and valleys of LapaLebombo were filled with the quiet but busy movements of many kinds of antelope. There were the princely looking nyala who, like their smaller brothers, the bushbuck, preferred the cover of the forests and riverine thickets. There were the impala, who ran like the wind and could spring three times their height in the air, and who often kept company with the sociable and amusing baboons. There were the waterbuck, who, as legend has it, once sat on wet whitewash and have ever since had a ring of white on their rear ends, and who often dashed into water when being chased. Also fond of the water were the reedbuck, whose tails held high in flight looked like bobbing white flags in the long grass of the vleis (marshes) and swamps.

And there were blue wildebeest who liked to roll around in their own dung, marking their territories like the rhinoceroses did; and the much smaller but delightful antelopes, such as the klipspringer, suni, steenbok and of course, the red, grey and blue duikers.

Often to be seen with the various buck were zebra and giraffe. Nature had seen to it that along with the tans, greys, blues, browns, beiges, reds, yellows and flashes of white of the antelope, the colouring and design of two creatures would stand distinct from all the rest. The zebra had unmistakable coats of black and white stripes, looking for all the world like horses in stripy bodysuits, while the giraffe had necks longer than the rest of their bodies and dark patches of brown on cream that reminded the Wild Ones of tortoiseshell patterns and honeycomb cells.

One crisp autumn day following the summer of good rains, a herd of about twenty impala were grazing near a grove of trees filled with chattering vervet monkeys and grunting baboons. There was a sudden shriek from one of the apes on a topmost branch. Within seconds, the baby monkeys playing

The impala froze as one or two males sneezed an alarm and lifted their nostrils to the air.

on the ground had been scooped up into the trees by their mothers, and breathless silence fell on the crowd. The impala froze as one or two males sneezed an alarm and lifted their nostrils to the air, trying to find the direction of the danger.

Intense with curiosity, the monkeys leaped up to the branches from where the first warning cry had come, and gazed out over the veld. Quite some way in the distance, picking their way carefully along a path trodden through the long grass by countless hooves, were two humans, or as Marshy called them, 'Two-legs!'

The animals were not to know it yet, but these two-legs were about three-quarter size, not fully grown, and one was female, one male. They were coming closer, the girl in the front speaking quietly over her shoulder to the boy following her. They were dressed in short khaki pants, T-shirts and sturdy walking shoes. They both carried large rucksacks on their backs and had various sized pouches strapped around their waists.

All at once, the girl froze in her tracks, raising her hand to stop the boy behind her. She pointed directly at the monkeys and turned to say something. As she did so, the boy caught sight of the baboons and impala and shouted out.

Hearing the voice of the strange two-legs, the baboons and impala both took flight. Only Papio, the brave young male in this troop of baboons, stayed behind briefly to bob up and down on his two hind legs in warning to the young couple. Uttering shrieks and other junglejabber, the monkeys also took off, leaves and fruit falling to the ground as they swung from branch to branch in the canopy of leaves. The young of both monkeys and baboons made their escape with their arms wrapped securely around their mothers' middles.

'Remember, you must stay calm!' the girl quietly told her

companion. 'Now you've scared away every animal in the area.'

'I know, it's just that I saw a whole troop of baboons, and they're my favourites,' replied the boy. 'Sorry, I won't do it again.'

The two young people smiled at each other.

'This is fun, isn't it?' said the girl. 'There's so much to see. Do you think we should set up camp somewhere here, or closer to the river? I'm just a bit worried about crocs, aren't you?'

'Let's walk on a little – it looks like there may be a good clearing on that koppie overlooking the river,' the boy suggested, pointing to a small hill shaded by a large fever tree.

Many of the impala and apes who had raced away had slowed their flight, some pausing to turn around and observe the foreign creatures. Their quizziness leading them on, Papio and several monkeys began to make their way cautiously back through the treetops towards the fever tree. When the two-legs halted on the crest of the hillock and shrugged the heavy bags from their shoulders, the animals sprang back in quick retreat. From a safer distance and partially hidden by the leaves of their tree, they continued to watch quietly.

'Ooh, this'd be perfect here,' whispered the girl. 'We're close enough to the river to watch the animals coming for water at sunset, yet high enough away to avoid the crocs, I should think. But you know what they say if you sleep under a fever tree, don't you?'

'You mean about going mad?' the boy answered. 'That's because in the old days they got malaria in the areas where fever trees grew, on account of all the mosquitos. That's why they're called fever trees. But we'll be OK. We've got plenty of repellent and you took the pills Mom gave us, didn't you?'

The girl nodded, and together they began clearing a small flat sandy area of thorns and stones, and then untying and emptying their bags. They went about setting up camp as quietly as they could, obviously hoping to undo the damage done when they'd first startled the animals.

As item after item came out of the bags, including a shiny looking pot, long poles and a huge piece of cloth the Wild Ones later saw ended up being a tent, or 'two-leg den' as they called it, the braver animals edged closer. The impala, who had been quite indignant at having to abandon their choice grazing, were also step-by-step drawing nearer.

Being in the heart of the LapaLebombo region, these animals were not as frightened of humans as some of their brothers were. Had they heard shots from a rifle or seen the spearing of a fellow creature before, they would surely have fled when the tent poles were being unpacked. And the little black boxes with shiny glass eyes that each of the teenagers took out from their packs would have scared them away too (in fact, these were only binoculars). Now they simply made the animals even more curious. The monkeys were particularly intrigued by another little black box which at one point the two-legs took out and spoke softly into. A sudden crackling and sputtering was heard in response, and then some other deeper-toned two-leg sounds.

When the two-legs finally finished what seemed to be the building of their den, they closed the entrance to their cave-like nest, and headed down towards the meandering river. The monkeys were the first to approach the empty den, some of the younger ones running on ahead of their mothers' warnings to wait up. In excited leaps and rolls, they quickly explored the tent, racing up the guide ropes and sliding down the side walls in glee. The mothers, ever on the lookout for things interesting to eat, prowled warily around a big square box. Although tightly sealed, it gave off the scent of fruit and something else the monkeys couldn't identify, but found attractive. High in the safety of the fever tree, the male monkeys kept guard, peering in the direction of the two-legs long after they had disappeared into a section of thicket lining the river bank. Papio sat alone in a nearby sausage tree and watched over the antics of the young monkeys mothers.

He could hear the movements and calls of the rest of his baboon troop as they made their way from the veld upwards towards the craggy slopes bounding the river valley on one side. He knew they were headed for a kloof that cut though the hills and ended at a sheer rock face. Here, a crisp spray of water plunged from a dizzying height into a deep pool and then sought its inevitable way to the large river, to become one with the rest of the mountain-fed streams that in old age finally met the sea. He thought about catching up with the other baboons before he was left too far behind, but the sun was still high. He felt confident enough of being able to reach their favourite haunt before night fell and the leopard appeared, whom the baboons chiefly feared.

No, Papio being the show-off in his troop, he saw an opportunity to venture off alone and find out more about the two-legs and their actions. Then he would have something over the more dominant males who were always pushing him into second place. He decided to follow the track left by the two-legs, hoping they had not yet gone far.

His ears and eyes straining for the first sign of the humans, Papio left the protection of the sausage tree and loped across the open veld between him and the river. As soon as he reached the riverine thicket, he shinned up a wild palm and searched the water course for the two-legs.

Using his keen eyesight and sticking to the high branches of the thicket, Papio was able to follow the two-legs' trail. It took him round a smooth bend in the river and to a section where the bank rose steeply into a tangle of dead bushes washed down in some previous flood. Here the tracks ended, and Papio's view further along the bank on his side of the river was blocked. The river had widened into a broad natural dam, and Papio could see from the many various animal tracks on the far shore that this was a favourite watering hole for all.

'Now where have those two-legs got to,' he pondered.

A sudden slight shuffle beyond the cluster of fallen branches alerted him to the presence of something on the other side. Very quietly, Papio began to climb on all fours over the dry crackly brush. A flash of colour a metre before him made him pull up short. There on the other side of one scraggly fallen bush were the two-legs!

Quickly Papio retreated a step or two and then raced up a nearby tree for safety. From behind the leafy branches he peered down at the two.

'Did you hear that?' the boy whispered to the girl. The two-legs were quiet as they looked around them, searching the thicket to see whatever had made the sound. Papio held his breath, and kept as still as a waiting crocodile. He hoped the two-legs wouldn't see the slight swaying of the end of the branch he had leaped on to. He wasn't really frightened of the two-legs, but he did want to watch them secretly for a while. After all, he was hoping to go back to the troop with something new to tell them about these strange creatures who had ventured into their Wilderness.

Meanwhile, the two-legs, whose names were Lindi and Paul, were talking softly to each other as they scanned the river with binoculars.

'This has to be the best ever spot for a hide,' Paul said to Lindi. 'Do you think Dad has seen it?'

'I'm sure he has,' replied Lindi, 'and that's why he told us to come camping down here. He promised we'd see more than we could hope for.'

'Well, this is where the hide should be, and the tree houses could be up in that grove of trees where we first saw the impala and baboons. And then the rustic huts could be near where we've set up camp. The tourists will love this spot. It's got everything – beautiful scenery, with the mountains in the background, river, vlei, flat walking trails, hills, loads of animals... what more could you want!' he exclaimed enthusiastically.

His sister Lindiwe laughed quietly.

'You're so excited,' she whispered, 'and we haven't even been here one day. There're probably hundreds of spots like this. No one except Mom and Dad has been through here in years. Wait till we've camped out a few more times, near the lake, up in the hills – then we'll know where to put the rest camps.'

Paul shook his head. 'No, I know this is a good spot. But we can look at others, too. When Dad finds those caves up in the mountains, I bet people will want to stay there. And there will have to be camp sites down by the swamps, and near the beach where the new turtle hatching sites are being established. You're right – there'll be lots of places. I just hope this deal comes off... it's almost too good to be true.'

The two lapsed into a thoughtful silence.

Papio was getting ever more frustrated. He guessed from their voices and gestures that the two-legs were talking about why they were here in the Wilderness. He wished he could understand their words, but to him it all just sounded like monkey junglejabber interspersed with snake hisses. He turned his attention to a nearby branch, which he saw grew out of a neighbouring monkey orange tree. At the end, almost within his grasp, was a plump, ripe fruit. He leaned closer, balancing on his two hind legs and clinging with one hand to the trunk of the tree he was in. He still couldn't quite reach. He tried swatting at the monkey orange branch, hoping to make it swing closer. The fruit hung tantalisingly beyond his fingertips. He was still also trying to remain unnoticed by the two-legs, whom he kept glancing at below him. So far, only a handful of birds had paid him any attention. After a few chirps warning each other of his presence, they had gone on about their business, satisfied that he was not searching out their nestlings.

Sighing with impatience, Papio recklessly let go of the tree trunk and lunged out. He did reach the fruit, but it took a tug to loosen it, and the pull drew Papio off-balance. Down he crashed through the tree, determinedly clutching the fruit in one hand and wildly grabbing at branches to break his fall with the other. He landed on the ground with a bump.

The two-legs, startled out of their reverie by the sound of breaking branches, leaped to their feet, clutching each other.

'Rhino!' shrieked Lindi.

The two teenagers stared at Papio, who in his disconcerted state could only stare back for the moment. Face to face they stood, humans and baboon, and afterwards, neither could say

He tried swatting at the monkey orange branch, hoping to make it swing closer. The fruit hung tantalisingly beyond his fingertips. The two-legs were just below.

who had been the more alarmed. But it was Papio who first sprang into action. Still holding his prize tightly to his chest, he loped off in the direction of the nearest tall trees, and from there raced his way back upriver, swinging from branch to branch without a backward glance. Only when he reached the point at which he would take a shortcut away from the river and through the veld towards the baboon kloof, did he pause for breath. Looking back downriver, he saw he had not been followed.

Noting the lengthening shadows as the sun began to sink behind the mountains, he took only a few hurried bites of the fruit he had coveted so dearly. Then, shuddering, he tossed it aside and headed for home, wishing he was already there.

At the riverside, the mood was different. Laughing with the relief that comes after a huge scare, the teenagers leaned against each other for support.

'We're frightening away all the game,' chortled Paul.

'I don't care.' Lindi wiped the tears from her eyes. 'It's not often you think a one-tonne black rhino has taken a sudden dislike to you... and that baboon's face!' And she began giggling again.

'Come on.' Paul tugged at her sleeve. 'We'd better get back to the campsite and get some firewood before it's too dark. We can come back later, and see some animals drinking at sunset – if we can be quiet enough, that is.'

Together, Paul and Lindi left the river's edge, and ignoring their earlier route, cut a shorter path directly through the veld and back to the tall fever tree and their tent.

Although Papio was not able to understand them, the two-legs had indeed been discussing something very important, which explained why they had suddenly come to LapaLebombo. Over the years since the terrible time of an attempted tsetse fly wipe-out, some humans had realised the importance of saving land for the protection of the Wild Ones. Little by little, concerned people had bought small pockets of land in the area which were set aside just for the use of the animals. They were fenced all around, although those animals inside did not realise this was for their protection. Many of the larger Wild Ones often jumped the fences, intent on roaming free. The smaller creatures crept in and out of the fences, not liking them, but not being stopped by them.

There were also some fenced-in areas where Wild Ones lived but were not protected. Every time the seasons came around full circle, two-legs and their fire sticks would appear again, shooting at some of the strongest and wisest of the animals, and often wounding the others. And from time to time, two-legs with traps would creep through the night, leaving wicked wires and ropes that caught some of the Wild

Ones and held them until they died or were found by the two-legs and then killed and taken away. Worse still, occasionally one of their kind would be wounded, have parts of his body cut off, and be left to die. That awful fate was usually reserved for the animals with the strongest horns, like the rhinos, and the largest beasts of the Wilderness, the elephants.

But now something very exciting concerning the future of the animals was afoot. The humans who had been meeting in the cities in the south had come to an agreement with all the humans who owned or controlled land in LapaLebombo. They had decided it would be good for all of them, as well as for the animals of course, if they dropped the fences separating their properties and joined together to protect the land and its inhabitants. They agreed also that hunting in the area would come to an end, and that people with expert knowledge of the needs of the animals would be put in charge of protecting the land.

According to the plan, the whole of LapaLebombo, from coast to mountains, lakes to northern reserves, would become one large animal paradise. A few humans could still live there, but the animals and their safety would come first!

Paul and Lindi were the son and daughter of one of the first conservation officers to be put in charge of this section of LapaLebombo, which was one of the most beautiful and rich in wildlife. It included one of the largest reserves where so far many animals had thrived, and stretched east all the way to Turtle Beach. Its western boundary was high in the Lebombo mountains, and the caves that Paul had referred to were located in Ghost Mountain itself.

Both humans and Wild Ones claimed to have seen strange lights and flickering fires on Ghost Mountain at night, and to have heard unworldly noises and calls coming from its depths. The animals knew that many years ago a tribal chief and his successors had been buried in a special cave in the mountain and, sensing something strange about the place, they all stayed away.

All that is, except the scary mamba. While mountain reedbuck, klipspringer and red rock rabbits played in the mountain air, and blue duiker found safe thickets for their offspring up on the slopes, only the black mamba had the courage to slither in and out of the burial cave of Ghost Mountain.

Why did the black mamba grow so long – sometimes as long as a giraffe was tall – and have a kill rate higher than any other snake? The mamba's venom might not have been the most potent (the cobras claimed theirs was stronger), but the mamba seemed to have more and to be everywhere. It would attack from up in the trees or down on the ground, and stay to fight when others would flee. The Wild Ones believed such power could only have been won by braving the caves of the living dead.

The Mozambique spitting cobras, who could shoot their poison the length of a rhino, were not impressed by the black mambas' feats. After all, they said, they hunted just as effectively but didn't make such a to-do about it. The python, on the other hand, didn't think much of either of the other two snakes. As Agrippa, one of the stoutest, most handsome pythons said, 'Pythons don't need poison, we just squee-eeze our supper to death and swallow it whole, never mind its size.' Indeed, the python grew even longer than the mamba, and took the largest prey, including small buck.

The most beautiful of all the snakes in LapaLebombo was the gaboon adder. His skin was patterned with triangles, diamonds and butterfly wings, and glowed with various shades of brown, cream, purple, black and pink. With fangs the size of devil thorns, his bite was especially toxic and the Wild Ones were all relieved that he was rather more scarce than the other snakes. He liked to snack on hares, baby monkeys, birds who lived closed to the ground and occasionally toads.

It was thanks to the colourful gaboon adder that Mother Jackal, or Ms Feisty-pants as Leopard Ngigwe called her, was able to return the favour she owed Ngigwe.

It happened not long after Papio's first encounter with the two-legs. One glorious evening, as the sky was ablaze with crimson and magenta, Mother Jackal ventured out early with her pups, who were now becoming quite strong and wise to the ways of the bush. She wanted to take them on a foraging expedition, so that she could teach them some of the finer points of hunting. She headed towards Leopard's Crest and the rocky outcrops above the cliffs where the dassies lived, knowing that many small mammals lived among the nooks and crannies of the rocks. Some of them would still be active in the remaining light of day, while others would be setting off on their own nocturnal quests.

Keeping her pups strictly at her heels and very quiet, she picked her way along a game trail that led through some fairly dense thicket which hid them from sight. Suddenly she caught wind of a scent she remembered only too well.

'Leopard!' she exclaimed, and stopped in her tracks, the little ones colliding into her hind legs. She stood there, hair bristling and nostrils quivering, scanning the air for the source of the scent. Being the bold jackal she was, she crept forward stealthily, instead of turning back with her pups. Where was that leopard? She might even be able to teach the pups a few lessons in the theft of a kill, or at least its remains.

A general hush fell over the thicket, the birds either gone to roost or waiting in silent watchfulness for the two predators to pass by. The night-time cacophony of crickets, frogs and other choristers had not yet begun, and it seemed as though even the leaves of the trees were listening out.

The leopard scent grew stronger as Mother Jackal came close to the fringe of the thicket and saw a clump of rotting tree trunk and branches blocking the path. A thick carpet of fallen leaves lay on the ground, softening her already cautious steps. She paused to check the scent on the breeze, which was wafting her way from the direction of the mound, and to signal to the pups to stay back in the shelter of the thicket to watch.

With every muscle quivering, she inched her way around one side of the dead wood. There in the half-light she saw the leopard. By the thick cluster of black spots on his forehead, which she had seen at such close quarters before, she recognised Ngigwe. She quickly sank low to the ground behind a fallen branch to avoid being seen by the handsome cat, who was also in a stealthy creep.

Mother Jackal had seconds only to decide whether it was herself that the leopard was stalking, or some other creature. Remembering that she was upwind from the leopard, she figured he must be on the trail of something else. She took her eyes off Ngigwe to scan the area between them.

In the dimming light, she made out the shape of a small rusty-spotted genet, whose long striped tail was jerking strangely. The genet's head was thrown back unnaturally, and its glowing eyes were wide and glassy-looking. Straining through the branches to see better, Mother Jackal noticed the cause of the writhing genet's anguish. Hidden from the leopard's view, camouflaged in the carpet of leaves on the ground, was the sinuous and heaving shape of a gaboon adder, its jaws firmly locked around the belly of the genet.

Time seemed to stand still as Mother Jackal's eyes sought out the leopard again. She saw he was about to pounce on the genet, who no doubt looked like strange but easy prey to the hungry cat. She saw the adder jerk up its head at the sight of the advancing leopard. What with the shadows falling over the snake and the wind's direction, Mother Jackal knew Leopard Ngigwe could not see or sense the snake's warning stance. The setting was silent – not even a hiss from the swaying adder could be heard.

Unable to contain herself any longer, Mother Jackal let out an ear-piercing yelp, and leaped away from the thicket. The adder, distracted by the sudden sound and movement, struck out towards the branch where Mother Jackal had been hiding. Leopard Ngigwe, who was practically mid-pounce, seemed to rise straight up into the purple sky, paws flayed in an attempt to paddle backwards through the air. Only the poor genet lay still, his last breath escaping him as the adder's venom took its effect.

Leaping into the safety of a nearby tree branch, Ngigwe summed up the scene. He thought about the misdirected strike of the snake, the scream of the black-backed jackal, and saw the now motionless body of the genet. He realised how close he had come to a confrontation with the adder, and instinct told him he would have fared no better than the unfortunate genet.

His brow creased in puzzlement, he stared up the path after the jackal, who had long since gathered her pups and fled the area. Slowly it dawned on him. There was only one creature he knew likely to interfere in a scene such as this...

'Ms Feisty-pants,' he murmured to himself in wonder. 'Well

Leaping into the safety of a nearby tree branch, Ngigwe summed up the scene.

I never...'

And so it was that the plucky jackal evened the score of favours with Leopard Ngigwe.

The adder, in the meantime, had disappeared into the darkness, her belly bulging and skin stretched to bursting point. The genet was nowhere to be seen.

Several hills away, Paul and Lindi were enjoying one of their last nights out in the veld. They had been camping out during their school holidays, and as long as they remained in regular radio contact with the ranger's new homestead, they had their parents' permission to explore the area close to the river and their home.

There were several precautions they had to take, however. Humans had not appeared in this particular area of LapaLebombo for many years and several predators roamed nearby. The lions, who were behind the fences of the main reserve, were not an immediate danger, but there were others, such as Leopard Ngigwe, the hyaenas, crocodiles, and the snakes.

Like the lions, the larger animals such as the elephants, rhino and buffalo, were also within the confines of the reserves so the youngsters were not afraid of them. They were not predators, but could hurt humans if they believed they were threatened by them. But once all the fences came tumbling down, those animals would have free range over all the land of LapaLebombo, and camping out would not be so simple. In the meantime, Paul and Lindi knew they had to stay out of the rivers, keep a fire burning at night to ward off the leopards and hyaenas, and watch where they put their feet and hands so as to not disturb any hidden snakes.

After their first day under the fever tree, they also learned of the curiosity of the monkeys and baboons, who had left quite a mess after their exploration of the campsite. And the first night under the stars had been a revelation to the youngsters, who thought that darkness brought a general peace and quiet to the Wilderness.

After making a fire from dry fallen branches and cooking a string of spicy sausages over a wire grill, they lay back on a blanket between the fire and their tent to look at the stars before turning in for the night. To tell the truth, they were also a little afraid out in the Wilderness that first night. The faint sounds of living things in the distance were growing stronger as the light of the twinkling stars grew brighter, and the circle of firelight around them seemed to mark the depth of the area that felt safe.

Later, while Lindi slept peacefully, Paul tossed and turned, listening to some of the sounds of LapaLebombo by night. In the last hours before dawn, his fitful doze was disturbed by the 'whoop-hoop-hoop' cry and cackling laughter of what he knew had to be hyaenas, in the hills to the west of the tent.

'Oh no,' he groaned to himself, 'that's all we need now. A pack of hyaenas coming on a raid. I bet Lindi's left some food lying somewhere, and they'll be all over us like flies on ....'

But he hadn't even finished this thought before he fell asleep again. The night creatures of LapaLebombo were left to go about their business undisturbed, as they had done in times gone by and would, many people hoped, for all the time to come.

As Paul had heard, a clan of spotted hyaenas was in a good mood by the time the pink flush of a rising sun crept over the eastern horizon at LapaLebombo. During the early part of the night, the hyaenas had wandered around the hills, searching out prey in the moonlight, but without much success. Those closest to the southern fence of the large reserve had heard the calling of lions as they too had stalked the veld, and felt frustrated at not being able to follow after the lions, as is the natural habit of hyaenas.

Although hyaenas generally fear the big cats, they are skilled at closing in on them as they feast on their kill and then devouring any remains before the other scavengers make their claim. They are also known to be brave enough, if in a pack and very hungry, to chase lions away from a kill and steal the whole meal.

But that autumn night, it turned out there was no need to depend on the lions for food.

After spreading out in pairs or singly to search out their dinners, the hyaenas had finally met under a large acacia tree to compare notes. None had found anything to eat worth talking about, and all were conscious of an empty rumbling in their stomachs that was burning deeper as the night wore on.

While they prowled around each other, smelling to check that nothing was being hidden from them, the hyaenas heard a slight rustling in some bushes nearby. They all paused in their mooning about and lifted their muzzles to the breeze. They picked up nothing, the sounds being downwind from the tree. Back they went to their morose pacing, some snapping at others in irritation, others pawing at the ground.

In the bushes where the sound had come from was a large and once stately nyala bull. He was a magnificent sample of his species, with long sweeping horns, a deep chevron mark in white on his noble blue-grey forehead, and a long fringe of hair adorning his chest from throat to belly. His mane was tipped in white, and another fringe of reddish hair grew around and under his tail. His dark blue-grey back was ringed in thin white stripes and his legs were stockinged in yellow-beige. His name was Angus.

He had spent most of the day before browsing under the trees where the baboons and monkeys had shaken loose fruit in their earlier flight from the two-legs. Once the proud leader of a herd of five female nyalas and their young, he was now the cast-off old man of the local nyala population. One of his own offspring, a strong buck who had inherited all his good features and now developed reproductive urges of his own, had driven him off from the herd. Angus had passed the last few years as a solitary, but still brave and healthy, bull. He had accepted the way of his kind, and knew that giving up leadership was not a humiliation, but a passing on of responsibility. He was ready, if not pleased, to do so, and he enjoyed the freedom that his independence had given him.

In the last summer, however, he had found himself getting tired. It wasn't something he thought about much, but in the way of all Wild Ones, he sensed the coming of an end. And then he had stumbled into one of those awful wire traps left in the long grass by the two-legs, who in years gone by had ventured this far into the Wilderness. His hind leg pierced through to the bone above the knee, he thought he would never break free. Yet as the burning pain turned to a dull numbness, he found he could use his enormous strength to tear the wire from its moorings on a tree trunk. He limped away from the tree, the loose wire dangling from his leg. It was often to snag on other branches, causing once more the wrenching, searing pain that he had felt at first.

The days passed as the summer passed and, in spite of the illness he felt since the snaring, Angus continued to roam the bushveld, staying deep in the thickets where he felt safest. Only when something looked particularly inviting, such as the mounds of fallen fruit all around the campsite and beyond, did Angus venture into the open. He knew that with his injured leg he could never escape the chase of a predator, and how was he to know that the lions he heard calling in the distance were enclosed by a fence, and were therefore no real threat to him?

After feasting on the fallen fruit, Angus had gone back in to the thicker bushes on the hillside overlooking the campsite to shelter for the night. In the dark, however, he became strangely thirsty, and he yearned for the cool feel of running water on his tongue. He pictured the riverside, and his nostrils quivered with longing at the hint of water on the autumn breeze. But his nostrils also sensed the presence of the hyaenas upwind, and the breeze brought to him their yelps and chuckles, warning him of danger.

He stayed hidden in the thicket throughout the darkest hours of the night, moving around restlessly, trying to get comfortable, but finding his body ached all over no matter what he did. He wondered whether to lie down where he was, or to pick his way slowly through the bushes to the river. He had the feeling that if he lay down now, he would never get up again, and in spite of his pain he wanted to see and feel the river where he had once ranged supreme with his herd of does and their young.

As soon as Angus saw the moon set on its downward path to earth, and the dark in the east change to a pale grey that he knew came before the glorious dawn, he began a slow and rather clumsy trek to the river. While he was hobbling along, the wind took a shift in direction, and he no longer scented the hyaenas. Being not well and somewhat muddled by the ache throughout his body, he gave no thought to the fact that the hyaenas probably scented him now.

It was Sheba, one of the more dominant females, who first caught wind of Angus. Raising her head in exultation, she let out a piercing cackle, and whoop-whooped to the rest of the pack. Instantly they rallied around her, and she flung out rapid orders.

'Get in formation, you lot, and look sharp – there's something big close by and downwind. If we do this right, there'll be dinner for us all tonight!'

The clan gathered behind her, and she loped off towards the river on a path that would bring her alongside the source of her excitement. Thinking only of reaching the waterside, Angus paid no attention to the distant cries of the hyaenas, and continued on his way.

Within minutes, Sheba had her now silent pack of hunters in striking range of the great nyala bull. She signalled to them to close in on the target, and as Angus left the protection of the thickest bushes to cross a narrow clearing, she gave the command to attack.

Showing extraordinary discipline for such an unruly looking pack, the hyaenas leaped as one towards the bull. Those told to do so, made for his throat. The more junior dogs flung themselves at his haunches, and others fastened on to his legs. In seconds, Angus found he was so entrapped that his only remaining defence, his beautiful curved horns, were useless. He thrust his head about, trying to shake loose his assailants or pierce one with a horn, but all in vain. As he fell to the ground, he felt the grip around his throat become

And then there was nothing... Nothing that is, except the wonderful vision of his grand reflection in the deep waters of a river.

so tight that no more breath could leave or enter his body. With some satisfaction, he heard the yelp of a hyaena he had managed to kick with his good hind leg, and then there was nothing... Nothing that is, except the wonderful vision of his grand reflection in the deep waters of a river.

Sheba taking her first choice, the hyaenas fell to feasting, tearing chunks of flesh from the bone and lapping at the warm blood. They ate until they were full and then, under Sheba's orders, dragged the bloody carcass back to their clearing under the giant acacia tree. There they chewed at the bones and licked their paws, savouring the freshness of their kill and the roundness of their bellies.

In the large reserve to the north of the campsite where lions could be heard calling, lived a herd of fifteen elephants. They were led by an elephant cow already on her fourth set of molars, which meant she had two sets of teeth to go in her lifetime. She had seen more than forty seasons of rain and forty seasons of dry and had given birth to six baby elephants over the years. She was loved and respected by all the members of her herd, who knew her name was Thandiwe but spoke of her and to her only as 'Mamah', grand lady.

Her most recently born calf was Nandi, a female who at almost two years was ready to be weaned from her mother. Like all baby elephants, she had been able to walk under Mamah's belly for the first year of her life, but as she had grown taller, she had learned to follow closely behind, moving only to the front when she wanted to suckle between her mom's forelegs.

There were three other calves close in age to Nandi and, as all children will, they often played together and many times drove their mothers mad with their antics. Once during the last rainy season (around the time Whistle was almost washed out to sea in the storm), the four calves were wallowing around in a waterhole with the rest of the herd. Their mothers usually kept them close by, so that they were within easy reach of the shore where it sloped gently into the waterhole. This hot summer day, though, they were so engrossed in their own bathing they did not notice how the youngsters had frolicked off towards the steep banks and deeper water.

Not without a fair amount of showing off, the calves were showering each other with a fine spray of water from their trunks. Each would shout, 'I can spray the furthest, you can't reach me!' and the others would be forced to suck into their trunks as much water as they could and then spray it with all their might to prove they were as good or better.

Pretty soon they began to tire of that game, and looked around for a new amusement. Trailing down the steep bank on one side of the waterhole was a thick root from a tamboti tree.

'I know,' cried Nandi, 'let's pull ourselves up the bank using the root as a rope – like the monkeys do. I'm first!'

And off she waded, her trunk reaching the 'monkey rope' just as her head was about to disappear under the water. She wrapped her trunk around the strong root and pulled herself up the side of the waterhole, making it to the top of the steep bank after a lot of slipping and clambering for footholds that sent much of the mud under the root sliding into the water. The others were waiting their turn close behind her.

'Come along,' she shouted encouragingly from the top of the bank. 'You're next, Vusi,' she called to a bull calf below.

Vusi wrapped his trunk around the root and began to hoist himself up the bank. Being a bull elephant, he was heavier than Nandi. He felt the mud slipping away under his feet, and he pulled harder on the root. The root groaned under his weight. He tugged again with his trunk. With a snap the root broke, plunging him backwards into the water. Gasping, Vusi found his feet but was battling to keep his head in the air when Nandi, who had been peering over the side, came crashing down on top of him as the bank caved in under her.

The two elephant calves began squealing in panic. Their two friends, fearing the anger of their mothers for straying away, tried their best to wrestle Nandi and Vusi back to shallower water, but soon found themselves floundering too. The muddy water was churning with the thrashing of trunks, huge flapping elephant ears and flailing forelegs.

Wild Ones for miles around paused in their browsing as they heard a high trumpeting blast from Mamah which was soon joined by further blasts from the other mothers. The four matrons sprang into action, striding out to their babies with angry looks the youngsters were lucky not to see. Each fiercely grabbed her offspring by the tail, and yanked him or her back to the shallow waters.

Cringing with the indignity of it all, the little ones (if you can imagine elephants of any age being little) shuffled on to the shore where they stood waiting in silence for the lecture they knew was coming.

Mamah led the tirade, the other mothers agreeing in a growl that sounded like rumbling thunder. At the end of it all, the calves slunk off to wait under a wild fig tree while their mothers returned to complete their wallowing in peace.

'I'm getting too old for this,' Mamah muttered to her companions. 'May Nandi be the last of my children – my nerves won't take another!'

The wallowing ladies murmured their sympathies. That Nandi was a handful and always leading their little ones into

'I know,' cried Nandi, 'let's pull ourselves up the bank using the root as a rope - like the monkeys do. I'm first!'

dangerous situations, they tittered amongst themselves as they sprayed water over their shoulders.

Little did Thandiwe know much more was to come from her irrepressible young daughter. She was secretly very fond of Nandi's lively nature though and, dare she admit it, rather proud. For in Nandi, above all her other offspring, she saw the characteristics that would make her a worthy successor – as long as she, Thandiwe, could maintain her reign until Nandi was old enough.

After a period of good behaviour, during which Thandiwe relaxed her watchful eye over her daughter, the elephants ranged far over the reserve, plundering trees for food and tearing up massive amounts of grass in their hungry path. Other smaller creatures followed behind, feasting on the fallen fruit and leaves they couldn't normally reach, or snacking on the insects and other earth dwellers whose homes were exposed by uprooted trees.

Among those especially grateful to the elephants for their messy eating practices were the hadedas, eagles, owls and other 'meat-eating' birds, and the low-slung four-legged Wild Ones such as the antbear, striped polecat, banded mongoose and honey badgers. Those who didn't appreciate the elephant parade through their homelands were the creatures whose homes were ruined, like the ants, termites, nesting birds and even moles, rats and snakes.

The rhinoceroses were also not so pleased at the arrival of the elephants. The elephants didn't want to share their watering places with any other animals, and that meant conflict with the rhinos, who were also fond of wallowing and taking mudbaths. Since the rhinos preferred to stay in their home range, they usually waited for the elephants to pass through before taking their turn at the water, to avoid confrontation.

Coming up to a waterhole within a white rhino home range one day, Nandi was wandering ahead of her mother in her usual impatience to be first and see first. Just finishing off her drink for the day was an enormous white rhinoceros. She too had a young calf, who today was already on the trail back to the thickets where they were to spend the rest of the warm day browsing in the shade. While white rhino calves normally walk in front of their mothers, they usually stay close for protection. Today, though, baby Simon was a fair way ahead of his short-sighted mother. As Nandi headed over a rise into view of the waterhole, she came face-to-face with the rhino calf.

Nandi saw Simon first. The young rhino had his head down, grazing at some short juicy grass on the path while he waited for his mother to catch up with him. In Simon, Nandi saw a new and interesting playmate. She shook her head from side to side, her large ears flapping noisily, in a teasing display of the start to an elephant charge. Simon peered up at the grey shape before him, curious about the strange sound and smell, but made no move to join Nandi. The young elephant began to swing one foot from side to side, pretending to begin a charge. Simon still gazed vaguely at her, but instinctively took one step back.

Encouraged by the rhino calf's movement, Nandi let out a shrill blast from her trunk, and began a mock charge towards Simon. Alerted by the sudden noise, Simon's mother hastened her steps. Nandi pulled up some distance short of the motionless rhino, flapping her ears and trumpeting once more in an effort to get him moving again.

As Nandi headed over a rise into view of the waterhole, she came face-to-face with the calf.

Seeing the elephant, although only a small one, threatening her baby in such a way, the normally placid Mother Rhino was enraged. In a surprising show of speed, she raced around Simon on the path and charged headlong at Nandi. Suddenly confronted by a charging rhino twice her size, Nandi was terrified, too terrified to move. She dropped her trunk, closed her eyes, and waited for the smash.

In the meantime Mamah, attracted by Nandi's trumpets, had come upon the scene. She saw at a glance her submissive-looking daughter and the charging rhino, and flew instantly into a full charge herself. Just as Mother Rhino was about to slam her horn into the baby elephant, she glimpsed the awesome bulk of Thandiwe bearing down on her. She lunged away, missing Nandi by inches, and placing the elephant calf between herself and Mamah. Mamah was forced to veer away, but did so with a shattering scream of rage. Simon fled into nearby bushes, listening to the clash from safety behind a tree.

Still determined to take care of her offspring, Mamah turned herself ready for a second charge at the offending rhino. Mother Rhino, however, had had enough. Of a peace-loving nature, she wanted only to protect her baby. Now that she saw he was gone from the scene, she had no further interest in clashes with elephants, especially ones as fearsome in size and temper as Mamah. Looping her short tail over her back, she turned in her tracks and she too ran for Simon's hiding place.

Satisfied that Nandi was out of danger, Mamah halted her charge and turned to her daughter.

'Are you all right?' she asked Nandi.

When Nandi mumbled a small yes, Mamah continued, 'I am not going to ask how all that started, young lady, but let me warn you. The next time you tangle with rhinos, I may not be there to get you out of trouble. And the next time, they may not be white rhinos, but black rhinos, whom you will know by their pointed, not box-like, jaw. And let me tell you, my girl, a black rhino is a different story – much fiercer and less likely to give in. We would probably not be standing here unhurt if that calf's mother had been a black rhino.'

Mamah stomped her forefeet. 'You are no longer a baby, Nandi. From now on you will show more responsibility, and to prove how grown-up you can be, you will no longer suckle from me. Do you understand?'

Nandi's eyes flew wide in protest, but she dared not contradict Thandiwe. 'Yes, Mamah,' she said. From then on, she joined the other weaned calves in the herd to await adolescence and full maturity, when she would take her place as one of the leaders of that or another group of elephants, the largest animals living on land.

10

On the last day of their camping trip, Paul and Lindi had one of the most treasured experiences of their holiday, while the Wild Ones were treated to a sight they could not easily forget.

Having become much better at walking through the veld and thickets without alarming all the animals around, Paul and Lindi had managed to come very close to various animals during their stay. They had also learned to observe signs on the paths and in the bushes that told them more about the activities of the Wild Ones than they could have imagined.

For example, on the second day of their trip, Paul had taken Lindi in the direction of the hyaena cries he had heard that first night, and there under the giant acacia they had found plenty of pug marks but little else. After some skilful tracking, they had come across a small patch of clear land outside the entrance to an old antbear hole. There a clutch of scrawny-looking vultures were feeding on a carcass so torn apart and picked clean that the teenagers were at first unable to identify it. Only one long curved antler lying some distance away clued them into the existence of old Angus, who by then was just a warm feeling in the bellies of the hyaenas lying fast asleep in the depths of the antbear hole.

After packing up all their camping gear and stashing it in their backpacks, which they slung over the lower branches of the fever tree, Paul and his sister decided to take one last walk upstream before setting off for home. Walking very quietly, they barely spoke as they wound their way through the dense bush fringing the river. It was still early and cool enough for many birds to be on the wing, or busy underfoot, and they were thrilled at the sight of the hen-like Natal francolin, harlequin quail and even one blue quail. They also saw a large clutch of helmeted guineafowl who loudly protested the appearance of the two-legs with a noisy kek-kekking as they scurried away. In a flurry of spotted grey feathers and nodding blue heads, they moved more like panicked prisoners in handcuffs and leg irons than birds of the wild.

Brother and sister were picking their way down a steep and slippery gully, taking care not to step in any damp leaf puddles, or to trip on the many tangled roots and branches that grew along the forest floor, when Lindi caught a slight movement out of the corner of her eye. Silently grabbing Paul's shirt, she turned him to look into a low tunnel under some bushes. There in the security of a green nest stood a blue duiker, his body braced in fright. Behind him lay what was obviously his mate, and in the circle of her body was a tiny baby duiker.

Lindi and Paul stared as the baby nuzzled at his mother, who was gently licking at her young one's head. Some silent signal must have passed from the male duiker to the female, because she suddenly also became alarmed and, half-rising, turned to face the two-legs. The baby quickly but shakily tucked himself under his mother's hind legs. The entire forest seemed to be in a hush as animals and humans stood frozen in their tracks.

Moving as one, Lindi and Paul began to back away very slowly, almost as if they too had received a silent message: 'Leave them alone, this is their special place, don't frighten them away.' As they retreated, the female duiker cautiously lay down again and let her gaze return to her baby. Her mate remained stiffly watching, relaxing his guard only once the two-legs were well out of his line of vision.

After back-tracking some way along their path, Paul and Lindi paused.

'Did you see that baby – wasn't he just the cutest, most gorgeous thing you've ever laid eyes on?' Lindi whispered to Paul. And Paul, nodding, admitted he was. Reluctantly the two agreed they had better not go back for a second look, for fear of disturbing the family more than necessary, and they turned back for camp and their longer journey home.

Finally hearing the footsteps of the two-legs fade into nothing, Piti the duiker turned back to his mate.

'That was close, my dear,' he said to her.

'Oh nonsense,' soothed Petals, 'those two were harmless – I could sense it. I think they were just lookers, like all the others that have been to see us since Lilliput was born.'

Reassured, Piti lay down beside Petals and they both turned their attention to the baby, whose large brown eyes had closed in contented slumber.

The two teenagers reached camp, where they shouldered their heavy backpacks. They were just listing all the things they had seen and would love to have photographed, when a distant whirring hum was heard. The sound grew louder, and Paul and Lindi vainly scanned the deep blue sky for its source. Shrugging, they began walking the long trail homewards. Pretty soon, however, the smooth hum broke up into a thumping rutt-a-rutt-a-rutt.

'A helicopter,' shouted Paul. 'It must be Dad!'

In seconds, the two saw the brilliant white of the ranger's helicopter rise over the horizon, and they began waving, excitedly flinging down their backpacks and yelling 'Over here, we're over here!'

The surrounding treetops bowed and frantically fluttered as the helicopter, whose pilot had no doubt spotted the madly dancing two-legs in the open veld, dipped and swung overhead. It dropped lower, the engine roaring and blades chopping at the air, till even the long yellow grass was flattened below it.

Recognising their father, Paul and Lindi snatched up their

backpacks again and raced each other to the hovering craft, which finally settled down on a flat patch of bare open land. With heads ducked and clothes whipping around their bodies, they clambered into the passenger side of the helicopter. The aircraft rose again into the azure sky. After a quick sweep around over the campsite area, it set off south again, soon becoming only a disappearing speck in the distance.

The Wild Ones who had seen the helicopter flying overhead, and those who had been close enough to watch it land and swallow up the two-legs, were overawed and amazed. From open veld to thicket, riverside to mountain, the word passed quickly that a bird the size of a rhino with wings of a dragon fly and the drone of a thousand bees had preyed on the two-legs. Who of them, they wondered, would be next?

Little did they know that the metallic bird was not a sign of something to be feared, but of a great event that would shortly change their lives for ever.

11

The Wild Ones' unease over first the young two-legs in the bushveld, then the huge predator bird, increased during the next few weeks. Big noisy vehicles filled with two-legs began rumbling over the veld, stopping at various points where the two-legs would jump out and perform all kinds of antics the animals did not understand.

At the riversides, crews of workers scoured the waters for things washed down that didn't belong there, like the plastic bags and other human waste the crocodile Old Wily had noticed. Although the two-legs were taking the rubbish out of the rivers and throwing it into the back of their trucks, leaving the rivers cleaner than before, the Wild Ones were filled with fear.

'What if this means the two-legs want to come and live here, and take our water, and kill us all?' panicked the waterbuck. The other antelope – bush buck, nyalas, kudu, duikers and impalas – were all skittish too. The waterfowl and other birds of the waterside feared for their homes as they saw many of the two-legs stumble around on the riverbanks and slash at branches over the water's edge. They took off in squawking groups to watch from a distance.

'Just be thankful this isn't the height of egg-laying time,' breathed one of the geese to another, as they joined the jacanas in the reeds on the far side of the river.

The monkeys and baboons, ever curious, were swarming down the hillsides and river course for a closer view. Papio, having survived his close encounter with the two-legs (which he had described more bravely than he felt at the time to the other baboons), was bolder for the experience and led the way.

Other crews of two-legs, dressed in the green and khaki of conservation officials, drove up and down the fence boundaries throughout the range of LapaLebombo. They would stop at certain places, point to a piece of paper, then wave their arms in the air at each other. The animals weren't to know that the humans were noting which fences were to be removed and where the new outer fence would be built, all the way around the far reaches of LapaLebombo. For now though, the Wild Ones dreaded that more dividing fences were being put up, or traps laid, or that some other awful plan was afoot.

A few weeks after Paul and Lindi's disappearance in the helicopter, hordes of two-legs arrived at a central point in LapaLebombo. They gathered near the edge of the kloof so loved by the baboons. From the plateau above the rocky precipices, one could see both east and west to distant ocean and mountains, and in every direction the beauty of LapaLebombo was clear. To the south lay the estuary and broad riversides and to the north was a seemingly unending blanket of bushveld. Below, snaking through the lush ravine, was the silvery river that Paul was convinced should be the site of one of the rest camps.

The two-legs were dressed not in their usual work clothes, but in darker long pants and some in skirts and shirts. The Wild Ones who happened to notice this human meeting were worried. Lately, anything new disturbed them, and this change in dress was no exception. Word spread, and soon many more animals were gathered in the fringes of the thickets around the plateau to watch closely. A woolly-necked stork was sent to tell the larger animals who preferred to keep their distance, like Winston and Thandiwe, of the apparent change in tactics of the two-legs. Winston sent him quickly back, having told him to watch the gathering closely and report back if things began to turn nasty.

Amongst the two-legs, Papio spotted Paul and Lindi. They had not been swallowed up for ever by the 'bird-monster' as the baboon had thought, but were standing very proudly next to a man and woman dressed in those khaki suits that made them hard to see against the bushes.

There was a lot of chatter amongst the humans. The animals could not understand, but they sensed that the two-legs were highly excited about something. Their own apprehension deepened.

Suddenly, another 'bird-monster' was glimpsed over the southern horizon and its strange hum began to fill the air. As it grew in size, the sound became deafening, and the animals scattered in fear. Most retreated well into the thickets, and only a few brave souls, Papio among them, remained where they could see what would happen next.

This time, instead of swooping down and swallowing a couple of two-legs, the 'bird-monster' came to rest on the veld and spat out three large two-legs. It also stopped its thundering clatter, and its dragonfly wings ceased their dizzying whirl. Silence fell on the area, most of the two-legs

A woolly-necked stork was sent to tell the larger animals of the apparent change in tactics of the two-legs.

standing in the same quiet watchfulness as the Wild Ones.

Only the three two-legs moved, stepping over to a huge rock poised in precarious balance on the edge of the ravine. Covering the top and front of the rock was a white cloth the animals had not noticed before. One of the three two-legs grasped a rope hanging from the side of the cloth, and turned to face the crowd. The humans moved closer, leaning towards the rock expectantly.

The two-leg began talking in low tones. After just a few comments he waved his free arm across the expanse behind him.

'In the name of our forefathers, and of our children, and of their children to come, and in the name of those who have made this day possible, I declare the national reserve and World Heritage Site of Greater LapaLebombo open!' he shouted. He tugged on the rope holding the cloth in place over the rock. It fell away, revealing a bronze plaque with writing on it that the Wild Ones would never be able to work out.

'May the fences fall and the animals roam free, protected and treasured for all the world to see!' the man read.

There was an exultant roar from the gathered crowd of two-legs, and a flurry of clapping and flinging of arms into the air. With smiling faces, they began shaking each other's hands and slapping each other on the back. In frightened fascination, the animals looked on. Woolly-necked Stork hovered around Papio and his friends.

'What must I say, what shall I do?' he worried.

'Wait a minute,' barked Papio, 'something else is going to happen now. Look.' He pointed at a large box some two-legs had dragged off the back of a bakkie.

A second, heavier, box was pulled off another bakkie, and on the back of a huge truck a massive third box was shifted to the edge of the truck bed. A banging and rumbling sound came from the box. The animals pulled back in fear.

The two-legs took the lid off the first box. The air was filled with the soft beating of wings as thirty white-bellied doves rose up in an arcing line over the crowd. They circled over the plateau, then headed for the tree line where they came to rest. A cheer went up from the watching two-legs. The second box was opened. From out of its shadows sprang a young kudu, kicking up dust and snorting as it too headed for the cover of the trees.

Laughing with delight, the two-legs turned to the third box, which had been too heavy to move on to the ground. They were all shooed back into a line away from the box, and a long net was strung out in front of them. Two men picked up crowbars, and began prising loose the side of the box. The wooden side fell over the back of the truck with a clatter, and the men leaped back. Stomping and bellowing, a huge dark animal with thick sickle-shaped horns headed down the ramp created by the fallen wood.

'A buffalo!' oohed the crowd. The watching animals marvelled too. Not for many decades had such a beast been seen in these parts – the Wild Ones knew him only from tales they had heard.

The grey-black beast charged along the line of netting, then, kicking up his heels, stormed over to a group of acacias. He skidded to a halt and turned to stare at the two-legs. Everyone remained very still. Deciding that it was much more pleasant out in the open than in the box, the buffalo cast a warning glance at his captors, then dropped his head and trotted with a few grunts to some fresh, juicy-looking grass. There he stopped and began to graze, occasionally lifting his head to chew thoughtfully on his meal and make sure the two-legs were keeping their distance.

Only then did the two-legs dare move. Clapping quietly this time, they turned back to focus on one of the conservation officials. In a low voice he announced that the animals just released had come from a holding pen (boma), where they had been kept after being injured, and that many more of their kind would follow.

The two-legs then began to split up into small groups and climb back into their vehicles. Slowly the bakkies and trucks rumbled off and the helicopter rose up into the air, taking its three original occupants with it.

One bakkie remained behind. From his tree branch, Papio peered down into its insides. He saw Paul and Lindi again, with their parents. They appeared to be closely watching the buffalo, using those strange glass eyes he had seen before. Eventually they dropped the glass eyes and, after some discussion, also drove away, looking satisfied.

12

Confusion reigned among the animals of the region when news of this latest event was reported. It was soon brought to the attention of Winston, the white rhino, that a big indaba should be called, and urgently. Yellow-billed Kite and the eagles were sent off on daytime missions to inform all the Wild Ones of the coming meeting, and the owls were to make sure all the nocturnal creatures would be present. The meeting was to be held just before nightfall. A truce between predator and prey would be declared, and all the animals could meet along the boundary of the large northern reserve. Those who couldn't reach the meeting because of fences or other obstacles would be told what had been decided within twenty-four hours by the messengers of the air.

Exactly four weeks after the start of Paul and Lindi's camping trip, with the promise of a full moon that night, the Wild Ones gathered together for their indaba.

In his usual ponderous way, Winston opened the meeting.

'We are here tonight, er, or shall I say, this evening,' he began, his bottom square lip quivering with the solemnity of it all, 'to share observations on the activities of the, er, two-legs, who, er, seem to be invading our territory en masse.'

He paused, examining the crowd around him and making sure he had all their attention. He stared particularly hard at a group of mongoose and hares who were whispering among themselves. They were trying to explain the words 'en masse' to a pangolin, whose conversation was normally just a snuffle or a hiss when under threat. Sensing the rhino's annoyance, the pangolin rolled himself into a ball that presented nothing but hard scales to the outside world, and refused to unroll until the end of the meeting.

Once assured that he was being listened to with due seriousness, Winston continued. To the great relief of the Wild Ones, he speeded up his address, and shortly turned the meeting over to the various animals who had reports to make. One by one they came forward to tell of the activities of the two-legs.

When the Wild Ones realised from the reports that the two-legs were indeed everywhere in the region, they were filled with dread. The humans' noisy smelly trucks had squashed the homes of some earth-dwelling creatures and had bowled over several young saplings, destroying nests and beehives. The story told by the two owls, Marshy and Rufus, of two-legs filling their baskets with turtle eggs on the beach and taking them away, confirmed their worst fears. The two-legs would even plunder their young the minute they were born and their parents' backs were turned.

'We had no idea there were so many two-legs everywhere,' grumbled Shumba, one of the few lions of the region. 'It seems things have come to a turning point for us Wild Ones of LapaLebombo.'

Though seldom addressed by any of the lions, whom of course they usually avoided wherever possible, the Wild

Ones drew closer to catch every word. They had great respect for the largest of the cats.

Shumba consulted briefly with the other senior members of his pride, then cleared his throat (at which spine-chilling sound many of the smaller animals quickly retreated into the shadows).

'We see only one option left to us. Attack!'

The listening animals leapt back at the ferocity of Shumba's tone.

'Yes indeed,' said Shumba. 'We must all attack. Not each other, you fools,' he sneered at some of the less trusting Wild Ones, who were visibly shaking at his words and the closeness of the gathering. 'I mean we must attack the two-legs, and their rolling contraptions. At every turn, with every means we have.'

He turned to the rhinos and elephants. 'You fellows ought to be able to take care of the noisy smell machines. We and the other cats,' he gave a fleeting, begrudging glance at the leopards, 'can take care of the two-legs themselves.

'And you lot,' he fixed the cowering hyaenas with his burning yellow eyes, 'can do your usual mop-up operation – deal with the small stuff and the ones we miss.

'No doubt some of you antelope,' and here he couldn't help briefly licking his lips, 'can do damage during the daylight hours when we take a rest – I've felt the power of your hooves and horns.

'That is all,' he ended, being a lion of brief words. 'Except to say that we should begin tomorrow.'

There was a gasp from his audience. Winston, who felt he had somehow lost control of the meeting, shuffled forward.

'Now, er, one minute, Shumba,' he mumbled, while he tried to collect his thoughts. 'Er, yes, that's it. I think such drastic

'We see only one option left to us. Attack!' roared Shumba.

steps as you propose should be put to the vote, yes, the vote of each and every one of us. And we should at least have a few days to reinforce our homes and stomping grounds. You can be sure these, er, two-legs will be quick to fight back. Don't underestimate them – from the stories I've heard told...'

Here the giraffes nodded agreement. 'I think we're also leaving out something,' said one.

'And what's that?' growled Shumba, who resented any questioning of his decisions.

Unafraid, the giraffe, who was the female known as Camilla, went on.

'For one thing, at no point have we seen the two-legs try to harm us. Secondly, they do have tremendous weapons – those firesticks, which we have heard of and which kill with one bang. They could have used those against us, but so far they haven't, and we haven't seen any signs that they're going to,' she countered calmly.

'And, hard though it may be to believe, it is possible that they may just be here for our good. After all, from what the riverside dwellers tell us, they are getting rid of all the things that bother us.'

Old Wily rolled his eyes. He had been one of the first to welcome the lions' decision, imagining how delicious those two-legs would taste.

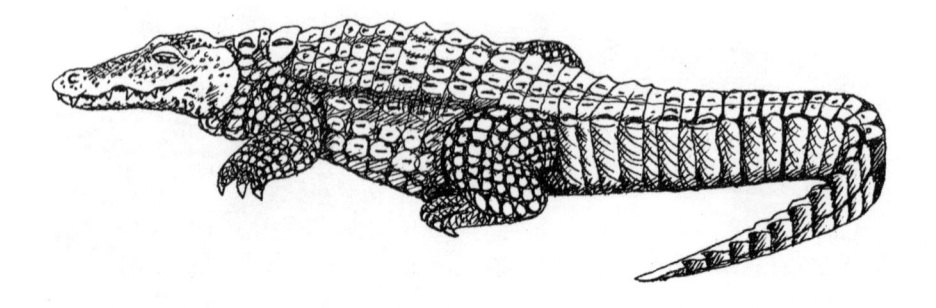

'Nonsense,' he snapped. 'Never trust anything with less than four paws on the ground. And don't for a minute think those two-legs don't have their weapons stashed somewhere. They're just waiting for us to drop our guard and then they'll take us all like plump sitting ducks.' He shivered with delight at the sound of those last three words.

The bird species, as well as the baboons and monkeys, were outraged at Old Wily's words. In their view, the fact that they spent more time on two legs than on four showed they were better than the other animals. The meeting threatened to break up in chaos as animal turned on animal, squawking and snapping and growling and barking.

'Hold on, hold on.' Thandiwe entered the centre of the gathering for the first time. 'Control yourselves everyone!' And she blew an ear-piercing warning note from her trunk. Silence descended on the audience.

'Winston is right. We could at least take a vote. Now, how many for an attack?'

'Wait!' All the animals turned to stare in surprise at Papio, amazed that he should have the nerve to interrupt Thandiwe.

'We've all forgotten about the buffalo,' Papio continued. 'If the two-legs mean to harm us, why have they released the buffalo and kudu here?'

'That's it,' cried Camilla. 'The buffalo! Papio, do you think you have a chance of getting him to tell you what is going on? If anyone should know, he should. I suggest we postpone the vote until we've heard what he has to say.'

The Wild Ones turned their gaze to Shumba, waiting for his reaction. Shumba's top lip curled. The tip of his golden tail twitched. The rest of the lions remained silent. The great lion's stomach rumbled, and he thought what a nuisance all this was – here he was hungry but he couldn't touch one of the animals near him, and everyone was arguing over how to deal with the two-legs. When lions are not on the prowl or in full chase of their prey, they are very lazy.

'Oh bother!' Shumba growled. 'If you want to be influenced by giraffe and baboons, then we lions will leave it to you. But you had better be right, Camilla, or you could have the blood of all the animals on your hands!'

With that he stiffly strutted away, leaving Winston to wrap up the meeting, which he did in his slow, but reassuring, way.

The animals agreed to meet again in two days' time.

13

Excited at the important part he had to play, Papio hastily made his way at first light the next day to where the buffalo was still grazing. Peeping through the leaves of a wild fig tree, Papio first made sure the buffalo was in a peaceful mood before he swung down to the ground and approached the imposing animal.

As he came closer, the buffalo stopped plucking at the grass and gazed thoughtfully at him.

'Er, excuse me,' Papio ventured, 'may I have a few words with you, Buffalo?'

The buffalo tossed his head, but said nothing. Although afraid, Papio came closer, knowing the eyesight and hearing of buffalo were poor.

Plucking up all his courage, he continued, 'Welcome to our land, LapaLebombo. I come in peace to speak with you, if you would just give me a moment of your time.'

The buffalo peered at the furry baboon before him, and slowly considered its nuisance value. If he did as the baboon requested, perhaps the baboon would go away quickly. If he ignored him, he might become an all-day pest, and he'd had enough of being bothered by creatures who walked on two

'Er, excuse me,' Papio ventured, 'may I have a few words with you, Buffalo?'

legs.

'What is it you want?' he bellowed at the trembling baboon.

'I, er, I shall be brief,' stuttered Papio. 'The Wild Ones of LapaLebombo have become concerned about the recent activities of the two-legs, and some are convinced they mean to destroy us all.

'But there are a few of us who believe they are here for our good, and we want to stop an attack on the two-legs. We were hoping you might be able to tell us what the two-legs are up to, since you, er, since you were brought here by them...' Papio's sentence trailed off as he lost his courage. It had suddenly occurred to him that the buffalo might somehow be working with the two-legs against the Wild Ones.

There was a silence that to Papio seemed to last for ever. Finally the buffalo swallowed a mouthful of grass he'd been chewing, and when he spoke it was in more gentle tones than before.

'I can't tell you exactly what the two-legs are up to, Baboon, but I can tell you they were basically good to me. I was wounded in the shoulder by some two-legs with fire-sticks in a land way back there,' he tossed his head to indicate the area north of LapaLebombo. 'I was convinced I was going to die, but the two-legs took me (much against my will at first, of course) to a place where some other wounded animals were staying. They prodded me and poked me, but as they'd done something to me that made my legs feel dead, I was helpless. I soon realised that my wound was getting better, and I was beginning to feel much stronger. I also noticed that the other animals were one by one regaining their health, and then were being set free. I became hopeful that I too would be released once I was fully recovered.

'Well, as you already know, the two-legs did release me - at least it seems I am now free. Only thing is, this isn't where I lived before. I was in a place known to all as the Kruger National Park, where daily hundreds of people drove by in cars on wide paths with hard surfaces. They didn't harm us, but seemed only to want to look at us. And we had a vast area of land to roam in, where very few two-legs actually lived. We even saw two-legs chasing away the ones who tried to cross our land on foot, and I've heard tales of two-legs shooting at those who came to set traps, or to kill us, as one tried to do with me.'

Papio listened in fascination. His fear of the buffalo was gone and he drew closer.

'Why do you think they brought you here?' he asked.

'I figured you might be able to tell me that,' replied the buffalo. 'Why were you animals brought here?'

Papio laughed, but very politely. 'We weren't brought here by two-legs – my parents and their parents and those before them were always here. We're worried that the two-legs are going to take us away or squeeze us out one way or another!' Papio quickly told the newcomer about the cleaning of the waterways and the patrolling of the fence lines by the two-legs, and also about the young two-legs who had camped near the river.

The buffalo looked long and hard at Papio. Papio stayed silent, waiting for the huge beast to speak.

'If you ask me,' Buffalo said thoughtfully, 'it sounds like the two-legs might be making a place for animals to live just like the one where I came from. Are there no other buffalo here?'

When Papio replied that there were none he knew of, Buffalo nodded his great head. 'That's it then... they probably brought me here to get the buffalo population started. (I just hope they know that as good as I am, I can't do it without a mate!) And this will become a new reserve for all the Wild Ones, as you call them.'

Papio pranced up and down on the spot. 'Do you really, really think so?' he asked excitedly. 'There are some places around here where we thought animals were being kept in safety, but we were never really sure. This place you came from sounds good, but do you think there will be enough space for us all here, as you had up north?'

'That I cannot tell you, Baboon,' grunted Buffalo, who was beginning to tire of the conversation. He had a lot of grazing to catch up on after his long journey. 'I suppose only time will tell.' And with that the buffalo turned his back on Papio and buried his head in a clump of sweet grass.

He need not have worried that Papio would hang around to pester him with more questions. Excited at the thought that some protected animal paradise was being created by the two-legs, Papio was dying to race back to his elders in the baboon tribe, and then the giraffes, to spread the news. He bolted up the nearest tree, and flew through the treetops to find his family.

The giraffes, meanwhile, were making their own exciting discoveries. Camilla and those who were patrolling the hills for signs of the two-legs did indeed come across some of their activities. All along the line of the large reserve where the fence separated many of the Wild Ones from each other, two-legs with various tools were taking away the support posts and wires and the fence was falling down. In places, it had already been rolled up and loaded on to the back of a truck.

To see what the two-legs would do, Camilla strode up to where the boundary had been and openly walked across, stretching her long legs in exaggerated steps. Several of the two-legs working nearby downed their tools and watched, breaking into smiles and even clapping. Perked with the reaction, Camilla walked back and forth several times over the old division line. Finally she was convinced the fence was gone for good, and the animals were meant to merge across it.

She broke into a gallop to bring the good news to as many of the other giraffes as she could find. They too had similar news, and the tall creatures were beginning to grow dizzy with the new feeling of open space. They swapped stories of the various animals they'd seen coming into their territory for the first time, and they speculated enthusiastically over all the fresh browsing sites they might find.

Papio found Camilla. Breathlessly he told her of Buffalo's prediction. Camilla was elated.

Dusk was falling by the time Papio found Camilla. Breathlessly he told her of Buffalo's prediction. Camilla was elated.

'It makes sense!' she exclaimed. 'They're taking down the fences so that we'll all have more space, and cleaning the rivers so that the water will stay fresh and usable for us for ever. And the animals they are bringing are to be protected, and to help re-establish the area with species that were here before, but their forefathers destroyed! Oh, I am so glad we were right. Our children will be safe, and there is a future for the Wild Ones here after all!'

Just before the last rays of sunlight left the sky, Camilla sent

Rufus, one of the oldest and wisest owls, to persuade Buffalo to join the meeting planned for the next day. Then, overjoyed, she settled her herd for the night. She was sure that their discoveries and the buffalo's story would be enough to convince the leaders that an attack was unnecessary.

Unbeknown to the giraffe, many of the other animals of LapaLebombo were beginning to feel the seeds of hope. The young kudu who was released by the two-legs at their ground-breaking ceremony had been talking to the antelope she came across.

Still shy and shaken from her capture and travels, she had quietly moved into some dense bushes where she stayed hidden for the first night and most of the next day. Towards sunset, however, she had been unable to resist the fresh scent of water from the south and had picked her way down to the river. There she had met up with the many different buck who frequented the waterhole Paul and Lindi loved so much. Among them were Piti and Petals and the fawn Lilliput, and also the impala, bushbuck and nyala of the area.

Standing on the soft, mossy floor of the riverine thicket, the kudu had waited while the others took their drink before joining them. Soon the antelope noticed her and, moving aside, indicated that she was welcome in their midst. They were all bursting with curiosity about her experiences and wasted no time in talking to her. After the usual polite formalities, in which the animals learnt her name was Nhoro, they pressed her for details about the two-legs' handling of her.

Her tale was similar to Buffalo's. She had been injured by hunters who succeeded in killing her mate, a beautiful buck who had sired the baby she was still carrying. Other two-legs dressed in green and brown uniforms had captured her and treated her for shock and the small wound she had in her rump. Then they had brought her here from a game farm nearby, which was to become part of the Greater LapaLebombo reserve once it had been cleared of the two-legs who lived and hunted there.

Nhoro also told them that while on her journey in the bakkie across the veld and through several farms, she had seen the dismantling of many of the fences. She had also heard of the one long fence that was being built miles away around the whole of LapaLebombo, just for the protection of the animals.

Although she had been shot, Nhoro's later experiences with the two-legs were positive, so the waterhole visitors were encouraged. They decided to send delegates to the meeting of the leaders at dawn the next day to vote against an attack.

That night, a greatly relieved pair of blue duikers went home from the waterhole. Piti and Petals had been in mortal fear for the safety of their new son Lilliput when the animals had called for an attack on the two-legs. Only the idea that the Wild Ones might after all be allowed to live in protected harmony could ease their minds. They wished with all their might that the attack plan would be cancelled the next day.

Sunrise the next morning saw a trail of various excited animals from several directions heading to the meeting of the leaders. The sky over LapaLebombo was flushed rose pink and the air was crisp and full of the promise of a new dawn. Not just of another day, but of a new future too.

As the leaders met in the lee of a giant kopje they'd picked for their meeting site, they were bristling with expectation. News had travelled fast through the night on the wings of the various bird messengers – the animals had important evidence they wanted to share. Camilla's long neck swayed from side to side as her gaze swept over the gathering and the paths leading up to the kopje. She held her breath, hoping that the buffalo would appear. She knew his presence would seal her case, but had Rufus managed to persuade him to speak?

It turned out the spotted eagle owl was as good with his words as he was swift on the wing for, soon after the leaders had gathered together, the buffalo sauntered into view. The animals made way for him as he walked up to the giraffes, who with Winston the rhino were waiting to open the meeting. Camilla briefly thanked him, then with a nod from Winston, began speaking.

She described to the animals what had occurred the day before, and invited the buck and the birds to tell everyone about the fences. When they were done, she asked Buffalo to describe the vast reserve where he was raised. The animals were elated to hear how huge and peaceful it was. When he told them he thought the same kind of place was being created at LapaLebombo, the animals were filled with the joy of creatures saved from certain death.

'I call for a vote,' cried Camilla. 'Are we to attack the two-legs or do we trust in their actions and look forward to a new beginning? A new place where we are safe and free to roam for miles, where clean water will flow and good food will grow, and our children will live to tell our tale!'

The cheer that went up from delegates and leaders at the meeting could be heard echoing in the valleys all around. With the agreement of the lions and even Old Wily the crocodile, it was decided a vote was not necessary. The attack plan was off.

With one mind, the Wild Ones turned to gaze at the eastern sky, now ablaze with the rays of a golden sun.

'We will live in harmony at LapaLebombo, we will survive,' they chorused. And, with a collective kick of their heels or swish of their tails, they split up to spread the good news to all the animals.

The land of LapaLebombo would regain its magic as a special place in the world, and it would be theirs for ever.

GLOSSARY OF CREATURES MENTIONED IN THIS BOOK

antbear Also known as an aardvark, has a long pig-like snout and strong tail (see front cover). Mostly nocturnal, feeds on ants and termites.

baboon (chacma) Part of the primate group of animals. Very sociable, living in troops with a dominant male as leader. Has a barking call. Eats fruit, fish and meat.

black mamba Africa's largest poisonous snake, olive-grey to brownish black with dark flecks. The inside of its mouth is black. Eats dassies and rodents like rats and mice.

blue duiker Smallest of the antelopes, very timid and seldom seen. Has a blue-grey coat and distinctive lines under the eyes (see front cover). Eats fruit, grasses, herbs and leaves.

buffalo The only wild cattle in Africa. Huge and heavily built, with thick horns. Grazes in herds, though single males are also common.

cane rat A favourite prey of many carnivores. It is mainly nocturnal. Eats grasses, fruit and crops, especially sugar cane. Lives near water and swims well.

cobra Rears up and spreads out its hood when alarmed. There are five species of cobra in Southern Africa, two of which spit poison.

cricket Grasshopper-like insect. Male makes a chirping sound with its legs.

crocodile Part of the reptile family: cold-blooded animals with backbones. Southern Africa's only species is the Nile crocodile, which can swim very fast and kills animals (and people) by pulling them under water and drowning them.

dassie Also known as a rock hyrax or rock rabbit. Looks a little like a large guinea pig, has no tail and a greyish-brown coat. Lives in groups and eats plants.

dolphin Part of the cetacean family: warm-blooded animals with backbones which feed their young with their own milk. The dolphin breathes air through the hole on top of its head.

eagle owl (spotted) Large, greyish-brown owl with ear tufts and yellow eyes (see front cover).

eel-catfish Also known as a barbel, because of the thick fleshy bristles (or barbels) around its mouth. Has a long eel-like body and special breathing organs so it can live in shallow muddy pools.

elephant Largest animal on land. Lives in small groups led by a dominant female (cow), or in groups of males (bulls) only. Eats a wide variety of plants. Threatened by poachers who tear out the valuable ivory tusks.

fish eagle Has a white head and breast, dark body, chestnut wings and white tail (see front cover). Always lives by water, but never the open sea. Has sharp spikes on the pads of its feet to help grip the fish it hunts.

flamingo Lives in lakes and estuaries. Has pink and white feathers when grown (pink because of the shellfish it eats). Feeds by putting its head under water and filtering food through its bill.

francolin Large brown speckled gamebird with a loud rattling call; rarely flies.

gaboon adder The markings of the gaboon adder help to camouflage it among leaves. It has fangs up to four centimetres long, the longest of any snake in the world.

genet Type of wild cat with a spotted coat and a long banded tail. Very agile and good at climbing trees. Eats insects, mice, lizards, birds and berries.

giraffe The tallest mammal in the world. Browses on trees and bushes, using its lips to pull twigs into the mouth and its tongue to strip the leaves off.

golden serval Long-legged spotted wild cat with a striped tail, similar to a young cheetah. Eats small mammals, mainly rats and mice, and generally lives alone.

guineafowl (helmeted) Large bird with a round body and grey feathers spotted with white. The blue and red head has turkey-like wattles hanging near its beak.

hadeda Greyish-brown ibis with long legs and a long curved bill. Bronze patch on the shoulder shines in the sun. In flight, gives a 'ha ha, ha de da' call, from which it gets its name.

hippopotamus Large mammal with a barrel-like body and broad head with huge teeth. Spends most of the time in water but also basks on sandbanks. Can be dangerous – never get between a hippo and water!

honey badger Also known as a ratel. Small animal, black on its legs and belly with a silvery-grey and golden back. Mostly nocturnal. Eats mice, rats, birds and reptiles and also raids beehives, using its strong claws to rip them open.

hyaena (spotted) Messy-looking dog-like animal with spotted coat and rounded ears. Will eat anything from insects to big game. Hunts in clans and also drives larger animals from their kills.

impala Commonly found reddish brown antelope with black stripe on each buttock. Males (rams) have graceful curving horns.

jacana Water bird with very long toes and toenails, to walk on floating weeds and grasses.

jackal (black-backed) Dog-like animal with white-flecked black 'saddle' (see front cover). Pairs stay together for a long time. Has a screaming yell ending in short yaps. Eats almost anything from insects to small antelope.

klipspringer Small antelope which walks on the tips of its hooves. Has coarse spiky brownish hair and lives in mountains and rocky places. Has a small rounded tail.

kudu Large grey-brown antelope with white stripes down its body. The bull has distinctive long spiral horns. Browsers which eat many types of plants.

leopard Powerfully built wild cat with circles or rosettes of spots over its body. Mostly lives alone. Active at night and in the day. Will eat anything from insects to antelope.

lion Largest of the African wild cats. Male has mane of long hair. Most social of all the cats, living in prides of three to 30. Females do most of the hunting but males feed first at the kill.

loggerhead turtle One of two types of turtle to breed along the beaches of northern Kwa-Zulu Natal, the other being the larger leatherback turtle (see front cover).

malachite kingfisher Beautiful bird with a bright blue back, black and torquoise head, red bill and reddish brown and white underparts (see front cover). Found in reedbeds by lakes and rivers.

marsh owl A medium-sized light brown owl with large dark brown eyes. Lives in marshes and damp grassland.

mongoose (banded) Smallish animal with stripes along its coat. Lives in troops of five to thirty, eats reptiles, birds, mice and other small animals.

nightjar Nocturnal bird with white markings on the tail and wings. Has a distinctive whistling call.

nyala Handsome antelope. Male is grey, with a mane and long fringe of hair from throat to hind legs. Female is reddish-brown with vertical white stripes on sides (smaller than kudu).

pangolin Also known as a scaly anteater. Covered with large brown scales, has a tiny head and large hindlegs and tail. Eats ants and termites. Curls itself into a tight ball when threatened. Mainly nocturnal.

pelican Large white bird with a huge yellow bill, with which it scoops up fish (see front cover).

polecat (striped) Similar to honey badger but with longer hair. Has black underparts and four distinct white stripes from head to tail, with white patches on face. Strictly nocturnal. Eats insects and small rodents, such as mice.

porcupine The largest African rodent with long black and white striped quills over its body which it raises when alarmed. Nocturnal. Eats plants, including bulbs and tree bark.

python The African rock python coils its body around its prey and suffocates it by tightening the coils when the victim breathes out. The biggest snake in South Africa, reaching up to 6.5 m. Often lies in water with nostrils and eyes above the surface.

quail (harlequin and blue) Seen in grasslands near water, the harlequin is much more common than the blue quail. The harlequin is dark brown speckled with white, with chestnut underparts. The blue quail has rusty-coloured wings with blue underneath. Quails look like small domestic hens in size and movement.

reedbuck Medium-sized antelope, brown with a white stripe on the forelegs. Lives in areas with tall grass near water.

rhinoceros White rhinos have square lips and jaws; black rhinos have a hooked, pointed upper lip and are smaller. Rhinos were killed for their horns and nearly wiped out, but white rhino have been re-established in game reserves. The black rhino is now an endangered species.

steenbok Small antelope with large ears. They cover their droppings with earth, unlike other antelope.

suni Small antelope with a white-tipped tail which it flicks from side to side.

termite Insect related to the cockroach. Lives in colonies with a king and queen. Produces termite mounds which can be seen all over the veld.

threadfin Small tropical fish with long streamers from its fins.

vervet monkey Has longish grizzled grey hair and a black face. Lives in noisy troops in woodlands and by rivers. Active only in the day and sleeps in trees at night.

vulture Feeds on carrion (flesh of animals that are already dead) and helps rid the veld of rotting meat.

warthog Type of wild pig with coarse, untidy mane, curved tusks and wart-like lumps (for protection) on the face. Tail is held upright when running. Makes use of old antbear, pangolin or porcupine burrows but sometimes digs its own (see front cover).

waterbuck Large grey-brown antelope with shaggy coat and white ring around the rump. Male has long ridged horns. Always fround near water.

wildebeest (blue) Large blue-grey antelope with maned and bearded head and fringed tail. Both sexes have horns.

woolly-necked stork Found near rivers, waterholes and lagoons. Has a long white fluffy neck and long thin reddish legs and bill. Wings are glossy black, while belly and undertail are white (see back cover). Solitary and shy.

yellow-billed kite Often to be seen along roads and near towns. Grey-brown bird with a yellow bill and a thrilling call.

zambezi shark Big grey and white shark which can reach up to three metres. Sometimes swims into river mouths. Unlike dolphins, sharks are fish, not mammals.

zebra Lives in small family herds on open grassland or woodland, feeding mainly on grass. Has a barking call ('kwa-ha-ha').